The author started out writing songs for the obligatory token rock band at high school. Most of these songs started as or became poems. As the author got older and became a trained nurse for the NHS, creative writing was replaced by essays and course studies. Then one day he became a father, with excitable children and vivid imaginations in the same room, tent, car. Stories were created from thin air. Phil Marsh started writing these tales down and on the many trips they made as a unit, weaved folklore and imagination together. All characters in his books are fiction but, in his mind, they are real.

To Mom and Dad

Phil Marsh

THE GIANT, THE WITCH AND THE RAINBOW

AUSTIN MACAULEY PUBLISHERS™

LONDON • CAMBRIDGE • NEW YORK • SHARJAH

A CIP catalogue record for this title is available from the British Library.

ISBN 9781787107021 (Paperback)
ISBN 9781787107038 (E-Book)

www.austinmacauley.com

First Published (2018)
Austin Macauley Publishers Ltd.
25 Canada Square
Canary Wharf
London
E14 5LQ

Acknowledgements

You have got to give credence to hearsay and rumour. Without imagination, the world would be a boring place. Fantasy, myths and legend, every story, fiction or non-fiction is based on some sort of fact. Be it a name, place or misheard gossip. Something must have happened, to plant the seed, which grew into the tree of a story. This story is based on the wilderness that surrounds the author at this present time.

Walking and exploring the rolling hills with his partner Sara, Phil has his own interpretation of what has happened to make these landmarks in Shropshire, Worcestershire, Herefordshire, The Black Country and Wales. Who is to say if it is right or wrong, fact or fiction? It might have happened somewhere in this world, an alternative reality, universe or imagination. Being written down has given it life, a physical presence to be shared by other people, not just rattling around inside the author's dusty brain.

Contents

Love

Without LOVE, there would be no life,
Without LIFE, there would be no world,
Without the WORLD, there would be no life,
Without LIFE, there would be no LOVE.

Prologue

A peach-coloured sky with orange-tinted wispy clouds dominated the panorama from the top of Cleehill. Black rubber caterpillar tracks bite into the grass as a roar of engine power moves the battered white digger forward. At the front of the digger is a bucket which is holding a large grey plate against a big rounded column. Sparks and hot embers fly outwards, silhouetting a welder who is fixing the plate against the column pillar.

"Hurry up, Mike, it's getting late." The moustache digger driver looked out over the horizon at the setting sun, thinking about a nice pint of beer at the pub. The welder pauses briefly and lifts his mask to quickly check his watch.

"No problem, Lionel, I'm on the last weld now." Flipping down his mask, Mike shouts, muffled by the mask, "It's your round anyway."

"What!" Lionel looks at the welder and catches a flash from the weld. Blinking, trying to get rid of the light line temporary burnt into his retina. "You prat!" Finishing off the line of weld, Mike pushes his mask up and back onto his head and admires his work. He looks up at the massive giant of a structure. The digger is dwarfed by the shadow that is given off by the structure. Against the auburn heavens, the pillar stands proud and firm. On top sits an enormous white ball; silhouetted against the sky it looks like a golf ball on a tee.

"Okay Lionel, we are done." The digger starts up and backs up leaving the plate securely fastened in place. Mike places his welding gear into the bucket and hops up into the cab, joining the driver. "Off we go then."

"Pint and a pie?" suggests Lionel.

"Pint and a pie," confirms the welder. The white digger manoeuvres around and heads down the hill with the two men on board chatting and laughing, happy with their day's work.

Left behind, magnificent in its size and stillness, is a silhouetted outline. A round mushroom shape stands. A perfectly round ball stands on top of a thick, sturdy column. It can be seen for miles, standing proud on top of Cleehill, Shropshire.

Dramatic skies add to its mystery.

The official story is that it is a radar antenna used by the military. But, as the two men know who have just left the completed structure, it contains something precious. An object, a magical object that is linked and rooted in the past. Its importance is not yet understood, as are a lot of landmarks round the border of Wales and England. To find out what is contained within this landmark on the horizon, we must go back in time, a long way back in time.

1

Darkness

The blackness was everywhere, thick, dense and totally impenetrable. It was the murkiness you can feel. Similar to a thick blanket covering your eyes in the dead of the night. A drip echoed in the distance. A plip, plop of water sounded from somewhere deep in the shadow. Chilled whispers follow the echo. The dampness feels like it could slither underneath your skin. Making the hairs on the back of your neck stiffen. Icy frozen fingers massage the scalp and run cold down the spine.

The quiet is sliced in half by a high-pitched whine. A shrill pitch that echoes until it bellows out into a deep yawn, as loud as a lion's roar. The cavernous sound physically vibrates the air, the noise of creaking wood and rushing paper swirled in the blackness. A slap is heard, similar to the sound of a wet fish hitting the ground. Then the crunch of grit being padded on by great bare feet rebounds around the pitch black space.

A sharp knife of light slices its way through the black. A cool bluish light floods the cave as the wooden round door is rolled back by a large hulking figure. The light outside is coming from a wonderfully large full moon. Majestically crystal clear, it seemed to be sitting central in the clear night sky. The night was beautiful, with a blanket of stars blinking in and out of visibility. A glittering blanket with the moon looked magnificent and grand diamond.

The cave lay in the side of a hill, just on the edge of the magic forest. Far Forest, as it was known locally. The moonlight scattered its beams across the higgledy-piggledy rooftops, which form the shape of the nearby town. The odd angles made it look like a crumpled piece of paper. In the centre, a church spire pointed proudly upward, appearing to be in danger of piercing and bursting the moon.

The hulking shape exited the cave and came out into the moonlight. Setting the door back into its resting place, the figure turned and took in the view.

The hands were large, very large. So large, in fact, that each finger and thumb (on each hand) was as tall as a small adult. Each palm was square and rough with dirt; there were splinters the size of fence posts protruding from the tough skin. The nails at the end of each colossal digit were raggedy, chipped and contained enough soil to replant most of the potted plants in the town. The figure yawned again and stretched. The lion's roar came back again but, not with quite the same effect as when it was echoed in the cave. The giant sat on an old felled tree stump. Watching and taking in the view. During the night-time hours, the candle-lit rooms of the scattered dwellings caused an orangey warm glow, inviting and comforting. The giant pondered for a moment. Like his kin and cousins, he had a hunger for power and domination. While soaking his feet in the watercourse beside Mawley Hill he hatched a plan to terrorize and scare the people of Cleobury County and make them worship him, making him their lord.

Moonlight sparkled for a moment, the fresh white light reflected on the dew drop that had formed on the end of his bulbous nose. The nose was long and had voluminous nostrils, the size of dustbins. The dew drop ran; this tickled the bristle of hairs coming from the nostrils and threatened a sneeze. The giant shifted his weight and rummaged in the tattered waistcoat, which looked like cow hide, to produce a large patchwork handkerchief the size and shape of a bed sheet. It probably was a bed sheet but it worked admirably as a hanky, scooping up and absorbing the snot. Light glinted off the moist large lower lip which hung low towards the jaw, dwarfing the upper lip, which was smaller and drew back. The pair of mismatched lips framed a crooked, uneven set of teeth. Like off-white grave stones the upper set of teeth jutted out at alarming angles. Spittle was hard to contain with such an arrangement, so a tide mark of dry sputum could be seen at each corner of the mouth. Mid-way down the nose, folds of skin were present; like lava trying to escape a volcano these folds of skin seemed to be fleeing from the eyes. Bulging glassy eyes were set behind and under the wet bristly eyelids. The lashes swayed and sat against the pink flesh like cats' tails hanging down from a wall. The left eye glinted with a deep emerald green, ornate, almost beautiful. The right eye is opaque, a grey matt finish, quite dull. Both irises were surrounded by milky cream eyeballs. On top of the odd marble eyes lay one matted unruly eyebrow, singular. The hair on his head was a dirty brown, perched on top of his noggin like a runaway scruffy, spikey, damp otter.

The moon was full and the shadow of the Cleehill had past, so Cleobury town was bathed in moonlight. The giant decided this was his time. This was the first day of his campaign, the first day of his reign as ruler of Cleobury County. With refreshed vigour and relish, the hulk set off and stomped down the hill towards the town.

2

Attack on the Town

The giant used his shovel-like hands to scoop up large clumps of earth and throw them. The barrages of mud thudded onto the roads, blocking any escape out of the village for the townsfolk. The roar from his lungs shattered windows and warped doors in their frames. He ripped up ancient trees as if they were just weeds and tossed them aside. The slapping of his enormous bare feet on the cobbled streets sounded like whales being slapped by super-sized palms. The giant made his way up the High Street, causing a trail of destruction. Tipping up carts, picking up horses like a child picking up toy figures, placing them on top of roofs, just for the hell of it. He pulled one large rock from beside the main road and threw it straight up into the air. The rock travelled vertically until gravity took over and pulled it back down towards earth. The giant just glanced nonchalantly at the incoming missile. Just as it was about to bonk him on the head he batted it with the back of his hand, as if flicking away a wasp in summer. The rock hurtled, horizontally now, into the dark magical woods. A plume of lilac and pink dust showered into the sky above the wood from where the rock had landed. No one knows what damage it could have caused to the enchanted folk who lived there.

The hole where the rock had sat quickly filled with water. Long ago, a rock dragon had an encounter with the town. It had blocked the well up with molten rock as a punishment. That was many moons ago and most of the townsfolk had forgotten the well's existence, but that's another story. Removing it, the giant had restored the original well.

The giant seemed to be enjoying himself. Poking his finger through the windows of the taller houses and hearing the screams, it all egged him on. Dispassionately, the great feet of the goliath crumbled the gravestones in the yard of the church. The wall surrounding the church also crumbled, as he stomped and kicked it over. Suddenly, he stopped in his tracks. Clang! The church bell rang. The gigantic eyes swivelled in their sockets and fixed onto the church. Clang! The sound that was informing the town that it was midnight had the effect of enraging the brute. In what seemed to be a cyclone of temper the giant roared. Anger raged in the grotesque face as he loped through the church yard up to the steeple. Clang! THUMP! RIP! The hulking hands gripped the steeple and cleaved it clean off. Turning it upside down to see where the sound came from the giant looked like he was holding a gigantic cone.

Luckily the bell rope had snapped in the turmoil or the poor bell ringer would have been an aperitif inside the giant's new play thing. A circular breeze had started up and seemed to be emerging from the ground around the giant's feet. He didn't notice but, the whistling and strength of the tornado was gaining and expanding with intensity. Leaves and small branches were being lifted into a merry-go-round of a mini whirlwind.

"STOP WHAT YOU ARE DOING!" The screech pierced the mayhem and brought silence almost immediately. The entire town fell silent, save for the crackling of fires which had started during the destruction. The voice belonged to a beautifully dressed woman. Her thick brown hair gave off hints of bronze and chocolate highlights. A fire started in one of the cottages. "Put that fire out NOW!"

The voice was so influential that the giant scooped up a load of water from the now full well and poured it over the burning building. That done, the giant seemed to shake off the temporary bewitchment and remember what he was here for, terrorizing the village.

"Who are you? Who are you to question the mighty Bradnock?"

"I," replied the sultry voice, cool as a cucumber, "am Shiara, local wise woman. I live here. What do you think you are doing?" Bradnock starred straight into the chocolate brown eyes that illuminated Shiara's pretty face. The coolness and direct calm of her stare seemed to unnerve Bradnock. Even though he towered above her, he felt an internal power that the lady in front of him held. The giant straightened up, with the church roof still in his hand.

"I am Bradnock the mighty. I will be your lord and master from now on. You must all serve and obey me." The villagers shuffled and cowered, huddled together for comfort and fear. Shiara stepped forward, showing no sign of fear.

"How do you suppose you are going to do that?" A large cat slinked away from the crowd and encircled through and around Shiara's legs. The cat had pointy ears and was a smooth blonde colour. Its hair was speckled in places with a similar brown that matched Shiara's hair colour. It padded forward and sat proudly in front of Shiara, as if guarding her.

"By fear or by punishment. You all will obey me or I will kill you all."

The silence was broken by a giggle that manifested itself into laughter. Bradnock glared down at the source of the amusement; it was Shiara.

"You really are silly, haven't you heard?" The giant looked puzzled.

"Heard of what? What do you mean? Explain yourself, woman."

"No one follows a dictator anymore. That is old-fashioned." Shiara paced confidently. "Old hat." Staring Bradnock squarely in the eye, Shiara continued. "People want a hero, someone to look up to. Not a sour puss who just tells them what to do." She increased her passion. "The giants of old were worshipped for their feats of strength and the help they gave us mere humans, in times of need. Why do you think the giant race has diminished over the centuries?" Bradnock looked around for help; when no answer came he looked down at his bare feet.

"I don't know... is it because we don't have relationships?" Shiara looked up at him with an incline of empathy.

"That could be part of it, yes, but it's because when the giants became power hungry they pushed all animals to their limit. So, over time the animals became annoyed and ganged up to overthrow each giant." Shiara looked deep into the giant's eye. "When the giant couldn't find anyone else to dominate they turned on each other. Even the giant two brothers in the north ended up destroying each other! Can you believe that? They were brothers." The giant shuffled uneasily.

"I know." He glanced down, looking solemn. "They were my cousins." Gasps and murmurs turned to silence within the crowd. The wise woman wanted to reach out and touch the giant. Bradnock's hand came closer to her. Her hand was about to touch his fingertip when suddenly, his big hand, quick as lightning, scooped up the lynx cat.

"OI YOU, NOOOO! What are you doing?" Shiara was visibly shocked. "That is Leonard. My familiar. My darling pet." The giant bent over towards the witch's face and breathed, "You find me a way of becoming a hero. In return you will get Leonard back, either that or I will break everything in this village to smithereens, starting," the hand holding the lynx tightening slightly, "with your darling pussy cat." Shiara stared right into the giant's eyes with fury and hate. Both sets of eyes stuck in stalemate, trying to bore a hole into the other's sub-conscious. Then calmness descended like a façade over her face.

"Okay, okay. Meet me on the top of Cleehill at sunrise and I will make you a hero." Her head fell as if defeated.

"No tricks, little witch or the kitty gets squished." Feeling smug with his wanton destruction the giant turned and walked away. As if in a way of mocking he flipped the church steeple in his hand like a bat and stuck it back in place on the church. Of course it was out of shape and missing a few tiles, but at least it was back in place, the twisted spire. Seemingly happy with his work the giant gave a mock wave and stomped off back down the road into the night, disappearing over the hill and up towards the dark woods.

The sounds of the giant chuckling away in the distance infuriated Shiara but, when a mew and feline whine carved its way through the night air, the heart strings pulled hard in her chest. She turned to the crowd and sighed.

"Try and rest easy tonight, please. We will get through this, I promise." She turned to the family looking at their smouldering ruin of a cottage. "Please, come with me, Mr. Robinson. You and the kids can stop in my cottage. I won't be sleeping tonight. I've got some preparing to do."

"Shiara?" the youngest and scruffiest Robinson squeaked. "Why is the giant picking on us?" Her eyes were as big as saucers.

"Well, he is a bit of a coward, really." Shiara stooped to talk eye to eye to the children. "To the north, it appears that Bradnock had two cousins. They lived up in Church Stretton. The two brothers had a disagreement over which half of the hill they should rule over. During the disagreement, one of the brothers hit the other so hard that as he fell, his body split the hill and made the gorge that is now called the Long Mynd. In anger, the fallen giant scooped up the biggest boulder he could find and hurled it brutally back at his brother. The standing giant tumbled backwards from the power of the stone, and crashed into a large hill. It crumbled, half burying him, knocking him out cold. Not content with that, his brother kept piling stones on top of the prone giant until he was entombed. The stacked rocks formed the Y Carneddau Tuon, the Stiperstones. The victorious giant sat upon the stacked stones to make sure his brother couldn't get out." The children huddled closer to each other, suddenly feeling the chill of the night. "He killed his own brother, so the chair has been nicknamed the Devil's chair. When the clouds are low and a thunderstorm brews, it is said that the evil giant sits on his chair and stamps his feet in rage at his dead sibling, causing the thunder and lightning." The children's faces were white in the pale moonlight.

"In the south, a giant terrorized the golden Wye valley of Hereford. Originally coming from Symonds Yat, he was a colossal giant who wandered day and night in search of riches. When he came across Offa's Dyke, he got thoughts of grandeur and domination. Rumour has it that King Arthur himself had an interest and investment around Offa's Dyke. Therefore, the king himself came to quell the giant's meddling. A vicious battle between the giant and the king followed and went on for days. King Arthur, with his last bit of energy, managed to catch the knee of his foe with Excalibur and the giant stumbled. Its elbow snapped the large slab of rock that lay beside King Arthur, who was now tired from this epic battle. Standing over his enemy the king saw off the threat to his people and land. Exhausted, the king rested beneath the slab and slept while the dead giant lay in the open, becoming a feast for birds, wild cats and vermin. The slab of stone is still there on the hill overlooking the golden valley, and is known as Arthur's stone." All the children had gathered from the village, excited but scared at the same time on hearing the tales that were being woven. Shiara was animated in her story telling. Arms gesturing, syllables rounded and rolled for effect.

"To the west lies Ludlow. It is the capital of Wales and the Celtic passion of Y Ddraig Goch is present in the town at all times. The Red Dragon guards her borders well since defeating the White Dragon in Monmouth.

Y Ddraig Goch is a fire dragon and one day she challenged the white ice dragon to a fight to the death. The White Dragon, being an ice dragon, had starved and frozen villages. Hearing of the persecution and bullying that the White Dragon had been carrying out, Y Ddraig Goch had had enough and decided to protect her subjects. She confronted the White Dragon on the top of the castle walls. The people of the village watched in terror, awaiting their fate.

Lunging forward the Red Dragon hit the Ice Dragon's chest with its horn. The Ice Dragon howled with rage and pain as the blue blood poured from its chest. It slashed back using his tail, hitting the Red Dragon's head. Stepping back from each other both dragons weighed up the blows they had just taken. The battle fell silent for a few seconds. Then unexpectedly the Red Dragon took off and zoomed high up towards the clouds. In an amazingly graceful forward roll, Y Ddraig Goch started falling back towards earth. In what appeared to be a split second, the Red Dragon straightened out and nose-dived towards earth like an arrow. In a flash, the red snout shot fire at the Ice Dragon. The Ice Dragon shielded itself with its wings, to protect itself. That was exactly what Y Ddraig Goch wanted the Ice Dragon to do. The White Dragon had turned, wings spread out to deflect the flame, which they did perfectly. Trouble was it left the White Dragon's neck exposed. Y Ddraig Goch sliced its head clean off using the sharp point of her tail. The Ice Dragon fell dead to the ground and the villages were free." The children looked on with terror and glee.

"The rumour that King Arthur is somewhere around here will have peaked her interest. Arthur's father is Uther Pendragon, Pen means head, and therefore Pendragon means Dragon Head." Moonlight lit up the astonished faces, all were focused on Shiara.

"To the east," she continued, "the Dudley giant had had an argument with the giant that ruled Birmingham. After a slanging match of hurtful remarks and very rude observations the two giants turned their backs on one another. Silence fell for a while. Then one day the Birmingham giant bellowed from the top of his tower, 'I am the lord of this land and the giant of Dudley is a mouse to me.' Obviously the giant of Dudley took offence at this, as it was apparent that he was clearly two inches taller than the Birmingham giant who was nine hundred and sixteen inches tall." The youngsters looked at each other, trying to work out how tall the giant was.

"Not able to think of a witty retort on the spot, the giant selected an enormous bolder and launched it from the ramparts, using brute force and anger. The stone rocketed through the sky and splattered the giant of Birmingham against his own castle walls. The force destroyed the castle and killed the giant. That is why there is no longer a castle in the middle of Birmingham, but the one in Dudley still stands. The stone that the Dudley giant threw is mounted on a pillar in a graveyard in Birmingham. In the ruins of Dudley castle the stone coffin of the giant still remains."

The adult villagers were now also standing agog at the story that had been spun.

"Bradnock, of course, knows all this history and doesn't want to get caught up in a feud with any other giants. He walked and walked until he came across the windy little hotchpotch village we all know as Cleobury Mortimer." One of the children looked up at the wise woman.

"Shiara?"

"Yes, Josephine." The wise woman stooped to listen to the youngster.

"Can I sleep in Leonard's bed tonight, please?" The child's large eyes and small face reflected by the moonlight.

"Of course you can," a kindly smile spread over Shiara's face, "he would like that. You can keep it warm for him until I get him back in the morning." The child looked reassured by this news. Then some concern registered over the innocent complexion.

"What are you going to do?" Shiara sighed and ruffled the scruffy lock of the head in front of her.

"I'm not totally sure, but I do have a sprinkling of an idea." With a wink, Shiara made shooing gestures with her hands. "Come now, off to bed the lot of you and please, please try to rest, it may be a long day tomorrow."

The crowd started to break up slowly. An unspoken disquiet hung in the air like a bad smell. Shiara stood hands on hips, looking up at the misplaced spire. Its sharp end and weather vane stuck out at an awkward angle.

"It does add a certain character," she said aloud to no-one. Her hand naturally smoothed the air beside her right hip. The hand should be caressing the soft warm fur of Leonard but instead there was a cool breeze. Her face looked down where her familiar should be and sadly she bit her lip. Her eyes focused past her hand, noticing a bunch of bluebells growing out of the grass below. Near them were daffodils, the petals looking white in the moonlight.

"Bulbs!" she exclaimed. Kneeling beside the flowers, she said it again. "Bulbs, by Jove I think I know what I'm going to do." Excitedly she sprang to her feet and sprinted towards the back of her quaint cottage beside the church.

"What are you going to do?" a young man in a long white night gown and unfastened boots asked, as Shiara whizzed past.

"The answer! I think, I hope!" Then she was gone, into the blackness behind the black and white timbered cottage. The young man saw a yellowish flame ignite behind the property and the crackle and scent of firewood drifted across the graveyard. The young man turned and spoke to a plump woman who looked like she had dressed in a hurry as well.

"Looks like Shiara will be burning the candle at both ends tonight." The woman forced a smile. "Hopefully she will have the answer or we could be at that giant's beck and call, forever." The young man shivered at the thought as they were walking back to their abodes.

"How long do giants live for any way?" The questions continued as the villagers retired to their homes. Restless and unsettled, not many villagers slept that night. Least of all, Shiara. As the night drew on the fire beneath her cauldron raged and boiled, getting more intense with each minute. Sweat and concentration on her face, she was trying to create the answer.

3

Hubble Bubble

The orange and red glow from the beating flames cast odd, flickering shapes around the garden. With the darkness and the circle of trees that made up the perimeter of the plot, the garden felt strange. It looked like some unnerving disjointed figures dancing amongst the foliage, darting in and out of the undergrowth. Occasional sparks erupted from the fire, like sprites breaking free and rocketing into the night. Shiara's elongated shadow stretched up tall against the cottage's two-tone walls. She was busy, her arms moved at one hundred miles an hour, stirring, pinching and blending herbs into the large pot-bellied cauldron that sat stoutly on top of the fire. The flames licked and caressed its sides. Lots of energy was being expelled into and from the cauldron. There must be thousands of degrees of heat pumping into and out of the black pot. Not a hair of Shiara's head was singed. The flames appeared to avoid the hem of her skirt. As she sashayed around the cauldron, the flames ducked, bobbed and weaved, avoiding her legs and garments. The pot and blaze were under her enchantment, so they knew not to harm the lady or there would be hell to pay.

For this is the famous pot, Pair Dadeni or the Cauldron of Rebirth. A mythical cauldron whose magic worked on freshly killed warriors. They could be placed into the cauldron and be returned to life. There is a clause, they lose the power of speech and some think they also lose their souls. Shiara rescued it from a dragon that was using it as a way to keep peace and quiet in its surrounding villages. The dragon would sneak out at night, abduct noisy people, drown the poor souls, place them in the cauldron, bring them back to life, then place them back in the village. The other villagers thought each one that was silenced had gone through a nervous breakdown of some sort. The trouble was as the villages got quieter, the more sensitive the dragon's hearing got, even a little whimper in the middle of the night got snuffled out with a quick dunking and re-animation. The animals on the farms were quiet as well which was the only blessing in the village, because the children did not know the sound of the screams of animals on slaughter day. This had given a notable rise in meat consumption for this area because the animals were silent the day after market or birth. Little did the villagers know, at the time, that with each animal that was brought into the farms, the dragon would come out that night and silence them. But, with each passing day the dragon got more and more demented with the constant disturbance. It got to a point where any sound drove the dragon wild. That's when it started to pick on the people who weren't noisy.

Shiara came across the villages long ago, when she was having a travelling year, broadening her horizons. This village was populated by the quietest people she had ever encountered. After a night there she realised why.

Shiara had wandered into the village one balmy, sun-bleached evening. In the middle of the village square was a circular wall which housed many different blooms and flowers on one side. Her nose told her what was on the other side of the circle; a beautiful display of herbs and spices, flourishing in the warm afternoon sun. Shiara grinned with excitement as her eyes scanned the assortment, noting the differing varieties and species. With the index of herbs stored perfectly in her mind she rubbed some of the leaves and smelled the aromas, each aroma reminding her brain of the sight, size and colour of each variety. She was lost in the realm of herb heaven and she did not notice that she was mouthing the names of each identified herb with such relish.

"You can help yourself," a soft-spoken blond gentleman dressed in a simple linen smock addressed her. "They are free to everyone." She looked up with a start. "Rosemary." She spluttered, caught out in mid-thought.

"Pardon." The man smiled and Shiara blushed.

"I'm so sorry, I didn't see you there." She then noticed a very pregnant lady sitting on the wall next to the man. "Oooo and you, how could I miss such a radiant, beautiful lady who is with child." Shiara was dizzy with midsummer madness and the sight of this loving couple made her heart jump. "Please excuse me, I get a bit excited around plants, especially herbs. Love the things. So much to learn. Smell, looks and taste." After licking her fingers, Shiara looked up. "Did you say they are free?"

"Oh yes." The young lady was talking now, honey tone to her voice, matching her hair colour. "All are welcome to pick and choose what they want. We have one rule. Only take what you need."

"That's a wonderful ethos, there is enough for everyone," Shiara cooed at her newly found friends. "How long have you got till baby is due?"

"Anytime now, hence the drink."

"Raspberry leaf with a hint of chamomile, it seems you know your herbs well." Shiara smiled kindly at the couple. "Is there anywhere I could lodge tonight, have you got an inn in this village?" The couple shot a quick glance at each other; they replied almost in unison.

"No, nowhere opens after dusk." They looked slightly uncomfortable. "You could stop with us if you want, it's not much but its home. You are welcome." Shiara couldn't say no. They were a lovely peaceful couple and they had welcomed her to stay at their home. They were in their mid-twenties and were pale and thin to the point of awkward. The most obvious thing was that the lady was heavily pregnant. Being a wise woman, Shiara was welcomed with open arms.

"I would be delighted, thank you."

"Please, don't mention it."

"As long as I cook you both a dinner." Shiara held her bag out in offering. The blond man helped the pregnant lady to her feet and they set off towards the row of houses nearby.

"It's a deal. We live at Small Brook Cottage."

"I will see you there in a minute, I'm just going to get some provisions." Shiara busied herself into doing what she was itching to do. She dived into the herb garden with much vigour, sorting, smelling tasting.

The evening went quietly and there was a tranquil air to the sunset. Once the plates and drinks were finished everyone retired to bed. Shiara, still wide awake, sat in bed reading and writing. Unexpectedly there was an almighty crash and a scream of pain. Quick as a flash she hurtled out of her room and dashed towards the location of the ruckus. She met the husband on the corridor trying desperately to shut and bolt all the windows and doors. "Whatever's the matter?" The man was paler than ever and sweating. Pointing at the door he spluttered, "She is having the baby!" A broad smile erupted across Shiara's face.

"Wonderful news! Let's get this special being into the world." The husband was looking more frantic.

"You don't understand, she has got to be quiet." His anxious eyes stared deep into Shiara's. Her face went from shock to joy again.

"Rubbish, I've never delivered a baby yet without the odd screech or swear word. It's only natural." With that said she bustled past the man and entered the master bedroom. The blonde lady was in obvious distress; pearls of sweat ran down and off her brow. Her teeth had made her lower lip bleed a little where the poor woman was trying to stifle the pain. Shiara rushed up to her and grabbed her hand. Caressing the back of her head she lowered the lady into a lying position, speaking softly to her all the time.

"It's okay, er... what is your name?" Their eyes met in confusion then smirks.

"It's Morgayn, sorry I never said."

"That's fine, I never asked." Both women burst into laughter.

"Shhhhh please keep quiet... please." The partner had reappeared, nervous as ever. Shiara turned on the bed so she could see them both.

"What is the problem here?" She paused and prompted him with a nod. "Nethred, my name is Nethred."

"Nethred, why do you want all this hush, when you know she is in pain?" Nethred looked guilty and worried.

"You won't understand. No one ever does." Shiara visibly bristled. "I won't understand until you tell me. I've experienced quite a bit, you know." Her kind eyes were beginning to become strained. "Go on, try me." Nethred looked at Morgayn and just as he was about to speak Morgayn doubled up in pain. Nethred cuddled up to her, looking like he was trying to share the pain and relieve her of her burden. Shiara laid them both down and prepared the area, ready for birth. She grabbed some towels from the side cabinet and carefully carried the bowl of water from the dressing table. "It looks like baby wants to make its grand appearance now. Like it or not." The cries from Morgayn came from behind a clasped hand. Shiara worked at the other end, encouraging and reassuring the couple. Nethred was supporting his darling wife but looked as awkward as ever. It seemed like everyone in the room had held their breath.

Time passed slowly and then a sudden high-pitched cry pierced the air. Shiara grabbed a warm towel and wrapped the new arrival. She used one of the towels to wipe the worst of the debris off the baby's face. In one swift move, she had cut the cord with the trusty Athame, tied it and delivered the small baby to the waiting arms of its parents. The comforting mewing from the child created a peaceful calm over the room. Morgayn and Nethred were surrounded by a rose haze of love.

"It's a girl," Shiara whispered gently. The tranquillity was enhanced by the sound of running water.

A trickle at first, similar to the drip heard from a cottage roof following a storm. Shiara felt calm and comfortable, she breathed in the loveliness of the scene. Nethred noticed the sound of the water and immediately stiffened. Morgayn sensed his angst and the tension suddenly roused in the room. The hairs pricked on the back of Shiara's neck, the sensation heightening her perception. "What is the matter? What is it?" She looked around the room, no shadows, no shape shifting. She couldn't sense anything except for the growing portent. "What is it?" she cried at the family. The baby finally cottoned onto the apprehension and burst into a high-pitched whine. The parents grabbed onto each other, protecting the infant as the ceiling erupted and water gushed into the room. Rushing water poured relentlessly from above, sweeping Shiara off her feet and dragging her into the torrent developing in the middle of the room.

4

Spin Wash

The surge pulled Shiara underwater for the third time. Around and around the room she went, being hurled about like a rag doll. Her attention was taken up with trying to locate the new family she had helped just create. Bubbles rose into her face from the raging torrent that was trying to suffocate her. As her head broke the surface for the fourth time she spotted the cowering family. They were perched together on the edge of the tall dresser. Relieved but now on her fifth cycle around the room, Shiara noticed the water coming down from the ceiling in a jet, two jets to be precise. The water was warm. Under water again, her mind was doing quick problem solving. Two jets? Warm water?

Night time? Cannot be a tornado, surely? It's summer, scattered rainfall and low winds. The starvation of oxygen started to affect her concentration. As she broke the surface once more she caught a glimpse of a black glossy eye above one of the jets. A blue horn poked out above where the eyebrow should be. "Oh my…" pulled under again but this time she was preparing. She knew what she was up against and she had fear on her side. With the fear she had for a newborn baby's life, the strength inside her increased tenfold. Her left hand was already in her bag and searching, her right hand was in her belt already clutching the hilt of her blade. Out came the left hand from the bag brandishing a cord with three knots in it. Struggling to get her hands under control under water she managed to lodge her right foot through the bars of the iron bedstead. Anchored, she was able to work the blunt end of the blade under one of the knot loops. Closing her eyes, she mouthed some words and cut the knot. A massive gust of wind came rolling up the hill to the village, blasting and causing a gale across the houses. The water jets stopped. Another wiggle with the blade and another knot was sacrificed. A rumble and thunderous storm started crashing around the sky.

Lightning flashes and a grumble reverberated around the sky, the deafening crashes shaking the ground and walls. The water receded as quickly as it came. Shiara was left knelt on the floor beside the bed, her foot still entwined in the bed stead. Water drained away from her hair and clothes, she was perfectly still. Suddenly and with a gasp she roused into life, unravelled her leg from the bed and ran over to the trembling family. Spluttering as she ran and still holding the cord with one last knot in it she worked her Athame into it and cut. Another flash of lightning and deafening thunderclap rattled the heavens. Shiara stumbled over to the cowering family. "WATER DRAGON! Why didn't you tell me it was a Water Dragon?"

5

Drying Time

The family was sodden but all intact. They were huddled closely together. Nethred's arms seemed to totally encircle his wife and new born child. All three of them were perched on top of the dresser. Shiara made it to them, still panting.

"That was a water dragon. What is it doing here? It is too far from the coast." Nethred had taken hold of his new born daughter as Shiara helped Morgayn down from the dressing table. He looked up from the infant. "It came about five years ago, one rainy night, at first it was kind and compassionate. It made sure all our wells worked correctly, protected us from drought in the height of summer, watering our crops for us. Then one night there was a storm to end all storms. The thunder and lightning came at the same time, instantaneously. Bolts of lightning hit everything and everywhere. The dragon tried to shield the villagers who had congregated in the town hall. The dragon had spread its wings out in full majesty and they spanned the roof to protect it from the barrage." Morgayn took up the story as she gingerly sat down. Shiara, remembering Morgayn had just given birth, rallied and helped her down, comforting and assisting the new mother.

"A deafening crash happened, it made the earth move as well as felling everyone in the hall. It was instantaneously followed by pure silence. Not a sound was heard, it felt like we had all gone deaf. Minutes felt like hours. We just looked around at each other not knowing what to do. Then we heard it," Morgayn paused, "the cry."

Morgayn looked down at her daughter and smiled as the infant was put back into her arms. The infant was nuzzling, so Shiara smiled kindly and helped Morgayn follow her motherly instinct and start feeding the baby. Looking back up to Nethred, Shiara prompted him to continue the narrative. "The cry sounded like a cow mooing, but for a longer time. I was one of the first to look outside of the town hall. The dragon was still covering the hall roof but its head was limp and hanging down, lifeless against the wall. It looked scorched on the back of its head and the horn from the right side of its head was gone, missing. The sky was a clear azure blue. You wouldn't have believed that there had just been a storm." Shiara looked dazed and saddened that the dragon had been hurt in the line of protecting people. "What happened then? The dragon is the same dragon we experienced tonight, I guess?" Nethred nodded.

"Oh yes it is. That was the mighty Ddraig Dŵr. We can only think he was struck by lightning and turned bad."

Shiara was puzzled by this, dragons are normally benevolent to humans and a few bad pennies have given them a bad name. As for dragons turning bad, that was rare, but not impossible. If the dragon was wounded they normally grieve for a while, repair the best they can, then either return to the place they were born to die or carry on where they left off. Shiara needed to know what was wrong with this particular dragon, not just for her curiosity but for the wellbeing of this young family and the rest of the village. The pink beams of morning sunlight were starting to peak through wreaked shutters and roof. She gazed out into the new horizon and appeared to be calculating, concentrating. She turned on her heel and faced the couple. "Where is the dragon's lair?"

6

Come into My Parlour

The incline up the grass bank seemed to be getting steeper. Deep emerald pasture, speckled with golden buttercups and small goats skipping around, leaping at each other. Shiara glows with the freshness of the air wafting against her face and the exertion of scaling the gradient. Just before the crest of the hill she could see the path described by Morgayn trailing off to the left. For a moment she pauses, stoops and digs out a root with her blade. The root is carefully excised from the earth and wrapped in a piece of red muslin cloth produced from the sizeable bag she has across her shoulder.

"Burdock, always useful, if not for healing it is very good with dandelion in a tea." Looking up, a curious goat was staring back at her. Shiara simply gave him a nod, wink and salute. "I'll be on my way now, Billy." Springing up spritely she was on her way towards the rusty path.

The path was a rusty coloured sandy trail that seemed to disappear around the back of the hill. As she put her foot onto the track the familiar crunch of gravel and the flatness gave some comfort not only to her nerves but also to her calves. Looking back down the hill she realised how sheer the gradient was. The view was lovely, the undulating farmland to the east, the dark dense tree tops of the magical forest to the west. Momentarily her arms zipped outwards vertically with the shoulders, eyes closed, breeze rippling through her garments, she felt like she was flying. Her spirit lifted as sunlight warmed her face.

Only minutes had passed but her inner energy had been recharged. Opening her dark brown eyes, she took in the view with a renewed vigour. Turning her heel she followed the path and walked the winding route. The path seemed to be circumnavigating the knoll. Her keen hearing and instinct was pricked. The mouth of the cave was near.

With discipline and delicateness, she tiptoed, using the grass side of the path to cushion her footfalls. A sound, not unlike a whinny of a horse, whispered from just in front of her. The cave opening was starting to be revealed. It set off a sort of optical illusion as shelves of grass and weed clung to the inner wall, therefore giving the impression that the cave was smaller than it was. As the silent wise woman approached the cave she could see a beautiful translucent blue scaled tail curled around one of the rock stacks within the cavern. The scales changed colour from whatever angle they were viewed from. It was quite hypnotic. The grotto had grass throughout the floor. This dragon likes comfort, Shiara thought, better take my time and be polite.

Silently she crept further into this dragon's den. The light from outside was catching the dragon's gorgeous scales which reflected luminous radiance into the interior of the cave. A magical ambiance of yuletide and the aura of enchanted sleep, the cavern was one of the most exquisite places Shiara had ever had the pleasure to behold. The further she went in the deeper and darker the colours became.

In front of her lay the enormous bulk of the magnificent water dragon, Ddraig Dŵr. The dragon appeared asleep but instinct spoke of caution. She noticed a raised platform to the side of the slumbering giant. Up she went with the grace and nimble toes of a Cornish pixie. On the platform Shiara gently removed her bag, laid it silently on the ground and slithered forward onto her front to peer over the edge at the dozing Ddraig Dŵr.

The beast was remarkable, it was pure poetry. Handsome scales, powerful but sleek wings folded neatly beside the torso. By the look of the barbs on the wing tips this dragon was fast as well as capable. The spines from the tail to the neck were flat and smooth, needed for efficient water movements. The muscular rear legs were tucked out of view underneath the quadruped. The front smaller legs were at an awkward angle somehow. She peered through the dimness and realised that the right leg of the dragon was draped over the right side of its head. Positioned to protect, the foreleg was covering the dragon's missing horn and right ear.

Pulling her bag up beside her, Shiara silently rifled through the bag, pulling out three items. The first was the red muslin cloth with burdock inside, the second was a wafer of fresh honeycomb and lastly, a brown paper bag. She busily started to prep the ingredients. Firstly she shaved the burdock root with her blade so the inner root was exposed. Then she split the honeycomb and dribbled the honey all over the burdock root, coating it totally. Finally the last, vital bit of magic. From the brown paper bag she deftly spirited out a cracker; silently she layered the cracker with the remaining honey. With purposeful resolve, cracker in right hand, honeyed burdock root in the other, she readied herself. Now on her haunches the mission was about to happen. Whispering to herself, "Right, here goes nothing." Flipping the honey cracker into her mouth, she launched herself off the ledge aiming to land on top of the dragon's head. The crunch from the cracker being bitten was enough to wake the sleeping beast. With a start it reared its head up to see where the sound was coming from. This action was ying and yang for Shiara who was still plummeting through the air. The positive side was the wound and damaged ear was exposed. The negative bit was the landing area she was aiming for came up a lot quicker than expected.

With an impact that exited all the air from her lungs, including bits of undigested cracker, Shiara, at least, had hit her mark. The dragon was not expecting a human to be spread-eagled on its head. Understandably it reared and tried to shake the uninvited guest off. She rode the dragon's head like a champion horse rider. One hand gripped onto the remaining horn, using it as a rein. Her other hand contained the honey and burdock which waved around like a dandelion in a gale. In what looked like slow motion, the wise woman skilfully inserted the preparation into the damaged ear and covered the hole left by the missing horn with her hand. Lying flat over the dragon's head she started to whisper a lullaby into the other intact ear. Ddraig Dŵr stiffened at first, not knowing what had just happened. Soothing melody surrounded him and the high-pitched ringing and constant pain of his right ear had stopped. He felt lighter and tilted his head to listen to this angel that had materialized upon his neck. Returning to his four legs and then lying back down, Ddraig Dŵr lowered his head back down to the ground. The angel continued to alleviate the pain with her calm song. Shiara slid off the dragon's head and stood beside him, her hand still on the horn hole.

Opening the large eyelid to reveal an opal black eyeball, the dragon could finally see his angel. Standing there with her hand still on his head, Shiara smiled and her head tilted to one side.

"Does that feel better?" A normal level of speech volume was used and the echo reverberated around the cave. She held her breath, the dragon didn't flinch. Shiara breathed a sigh of relief. The colossal eyelid blinked and relaxed. With that motion, Shiara took it as a good time to have a look at this wound where the horn was. The cavity was about the size of a fist deep and just as wide.

"Oh darling, you poor thing, let's see what I can do." Digging and fumbling inside her bag, "I bet the wind whistles through that hole something rotten when you are in flight. No wonder you are grumpy." She flashed a grin. "Ah ha! This should do." With a flourish, she produced a quartz ball. Perfectly round and crystal clear the ball gave off a wonderful form. She knew that the ball refracted light into a rainbow of colours when sunbeams met it. This is special quartz, unique in fact because it also refracted moonlight into an array of luminous fluorescent light. Shiara looked deep into the dragon's eye and murmured, "Relax." With those words the dragon closed his eye and she proceeded to lift the crystal ball up and pop it into the hole. The ball softly sank into the hole and mysteriously the scaled flesh began to close up around the ball all the way till there was no cavity visible. No scarring, just flat smooth dragon flesh.

Ddraig Dŵr opened his eye. There seemed to be a twinkle in it. The dragon sat right up onto his haunches, towering high, almost touching the ceiling. Then it slowly lowered its head in a show of thankfulness, a sort of bow. Shiara herself bowed slightly as a mark of respect. The dragon snuffled his snout about to the left of the cave and flicked out a black pot. To the dragon, it looked tiny but once it was next to her it was big, big enough to fit a person in. Shiara looked at the cauldron and looked at the dragon. Ddraig Dŵr looked sheepish as if getting ready for a telling off. Shiara just looked at the black pot and understood that the dragon had been driven insane by the injury he sustained while protecting the village. The wound was infected and must have really irritated and caused such irritation; enough to kill and reanimate people? Maybe so, delirium affected each animal differently. He may have thought it was a cure for noisiness, which it was, a pretty drastic one at that but, effective. Could a dragon understand human feelings and morals? Shiara was wise enough not to presume everything on earth had the same outlook, good or bad rules that humans have or perceived. No animal on earth was as violent or as destructive as the human race so how can they think they are superior. Shiara walked up to the dragon, that was still in a submissive stance, and kissed it on the snout. The dragon rubbed against her affectionately, understanding the forgiveness.

Slipping and sliding down the hill was fun. The sun had dried the grass so rolling down was such pleasure. Dizzy from the rolling, she took a minute at the bottom of the knoll just lying there, embracing the feeling of grass under her feet and the breeze kissing her cheeks. The sun dazzled and beat down onto her face. Her eyelids closed, she meditated, using the red orange glow of a perfect summer sun. A shadow cast over her body. Opening her eyes she saw the outline of Ddraig Dŵr. Vast wings outstretched, magnificent and silhouetted against the sun, he was heading for the town. Shiara grinned, picked up her things and ran.

Entering the town she noticed that most of the population was in the square looking up and pointing, some fearful, some in awe. Shiara pulled herself together and nonchalantly strode into the square, mingling in with the crowd. It was only when Morgayn spotted her that her cover was blown.

"Shiara." Morgayn bustled up to hug her, baby still in arms. "There you are. We thought you were killed and the dragon was doing a victory flight or something." Swapping the baby onto her other hip, "What happened?" Shiara tried to look relaxed and cool. "Nothing really, I fixed Ddraig Dŵr's horn and hearing and now he is all better." The crowd had cottoned on and was listening intently. Nethred's face was agape, trying to find words but he couldn't. Shiara pitched in, "It is okay, honestly. I'll prove it." With a quick look up she whistled two short blasts. The dragon paused in mid-air then nose-dived arrow straight towards the square. People screamed and scattered. The only people that were left in the middle of the square were Shiara, Morgayn, Baby and Nethred, who was still in shock.

Ddraig Dŵr slowed and came to a graceful landing just beside the gang. He nodded apologetically to the family and lowered the cauldron to the floor. It was full of liquid which was a slight off-beige colour. Shiara strode forward. "Please listen, Ddraig Dŵr has returned to you as a benevolent dragon. He has seen the error of his ways and will be here to protect and help you from this minute onwards." An older woman with a shock of white hair stepped forward, pushing a bewildered looking teenager forward in front of her.

"What about the ones with the silent sickness? What is going to happen to them?" The lady was clearly angry. Shiara calmly confronted the crowd; the dragon had his head bowed in submission again.

"Will everybody who has a friend or family member with the sickness please bring them forward and I shall treat them." The crowd milled and jostled, unsure until one brave woman in her early twenties carried forward a girl of five in her arms. Shiara took the weight of the child off the mother and reassured her. Turning and carrying the child, Shiara caught a glance from the dragon; she gave it a very scornful look. The dragon cowered away. At the edge of the vast black pot Shiara scooped a ladle full of the liquid and poured some into the mouth of the girl. A flutter similar to a butterfly's wings appeared on the brow of the child, then what appeared to be a wafer-thin flesh coloured moth detached itself from the forehead and started to flutter away. The girl eyes flashed open, then with realization that she was being held by a stranger she struggled and escaped Shiara's arms.

"Mummy!" she squealed, delighted. The mother and daughter are reunited in spirit again. The flesh coloured moth was trying to make a break for it until a steaming jet of scalding water swatted it out of the sky. Surprised, the crowd looked at the dragon, who seemed impressed by the shot, then started cheering.

"The families who have members affected by the silence moths bring the victims forward."

"It is going to be a long afternoon," remarks Morgayn, talking to her baby.

Nethred pipes up for the first time all day, "I'll get the tea on then." Morgayn gazes at him and smiles.

The next morning the sun rose to reveal a new dawn. The flowers freshly watered in the night by Ddraig Dŵr craned their stems to take in the new sunlight, opening their petals to embrace the rays. The goats were awake and frolicking on the hill and the cock crowed for the first time in five years. Shiara had woken up feeling tired but satisfied, happy that this town has ironed out its creases. Downstairs Morgayn and Nethred were fixing the shutters, the baby gurgled from her baby basket.

"Did you sleep well?" asked Morgayn.

"Like a baby in a cradle," answered Shiara.

"You two are busy."

"Well, I think this is going to take a while to fix up," said Nethred. "Still, at least we can make it look how we want it to look." The scene was idyllic and Shiara took great comfort from that.

Outside in the village square the cauldron stood, empty and alone.

"Right Pair Dadeni, how in the name of Pegasus am I going to get you home and out of harm's way." Hands on hips she stood pondering.

"I'll take you and the cauldron on my cart," Nethred spoke behind her, "it's the least I can do." Shiara spun round and gave him a peck on the cheek. Nethred blushed.

"That would be super. Thank you."

So that is how the cauldron known as Pair Dadeni ended up in the back garden of the Cleobury Mortimer wise woman. Currently Pair Dadeni and Shiara are cooking up a storm in her dark secluded garden in the middle of the night. The flames are still casting shadows against the shrubs and the trees. There is one shadow that doesn't dance. It keeps perfectly still. Tall and skeletal, the shadow blends into the trees behind. It bides its time. Only now are its yellow eyes visible. The shadow detaches itself from the shelter of the gloominess, peeling its black figure away from the camouflage, and positions itself right behind Shiara. A dark, slender hand rose, long thin fingers reach out to touch the back of Shiara's neck.

7

Shadow Dweller

Ice crept up Shiara's shaped slender neck, the hair started to stand to attention in a wave of frostiness. The chill made her shiver. She made one big stir with the ladle, dipped a forefinger in and raised it to her eye to inspect.

"Shanflax, if that is you? Please make yourself look presentable," Shiara tutted. "There are children in the house, I'd hate for one of them to look out and see a naked shadow dweller, no matter how translucent you are." A crackly broken voice emerged from over her shoulder.

"Oh my darling, how I would like to get my hands on that willowy collar of yours."

Shiara spun around with one hand on the pendant of her necklace.

"It's not my collar you want, it's my amulet and well you know it." Stepping forward she made the shadow dweller step back. "What gives me the pleasure of your company? Or should I say, what do you want? I'm busy." The semi-transparent figure put up what looked like a skeletal black hand to stop the wise woman getting any closer. "Hold your horses, don't come any nearer, I would hate you to get that pretty dress burnt."

The figure straightened up, raised its face upward, the yellow eyes closed. A blue flame grew from the area around the being's feet, throbbing and pulsing. Blue flames licked and flowed higher up and spread all the way around its torso. Immersed and consumed within the blue blaze, the being seemed to swell and shorten. The upper body filled out and became more solid. Leg joints bent backwards and its calves lengthened and brittle hair began to sprout out. Hoof cusps formed and raised its height slightly. Thigh muscles grew, bulking out and taking the form of a strong stag or deer. The rest of its torso bowed and was aiming to stand upright. Female breasts were formed, similar to human but covered in fur. Shoulders that were muscular and practical were evident, leather binding seem to be bound around each wrist and elbow. One golden nugget was revealed on the left set of bindings. The head had formed and a tousled mane of black hair tumbled down, covering the front of the creature, and the mane ran down her spine, mingling into the fur at the nape of the back. The blue flames receded and a dark-headed female-looking being was glaring eye to eye with the wise woman. The yellow eyes had not changed. They checked and took in the form of Shiara. The wise woman did the same.

"What do you want, Shanflax? It's not autumn yet, there are no deaths for you to shepherd," pausing again to stir the boiling crock pot, "or cause. Why are you here?" The new visitor shifted confidently to the other side of the cauldron, still facing Shiara. "You need help." Shanflax stopped, looked straight at Shiara, the yellow irises were being picked out by the flames.

"Do you really think so? I've dealt with worse than you, Shanflax, and well you know it." The shadow dweller touched her left thigh as if reminded of some memory. "Who sent you? You are not normally this far south in spring. Shouldn't you be up north playing with your barghest, Trammor?" Her stare was firm and unmoving. Shanflax found it hard to look away from her. With effort and then submission Shanflax bowed her head. "It was Elonar, she sent me, and she thought that danger was coming your way."

"Elonar!" Shiara was now hurling ingredients into the pot, "Elonar! The nosy cow. Just because she is a few years older than me she thinks she knows it all." Shiara changed the pitch of her voice to sound squeaky and girly. "Ooh, Shiara, you shouldn't be doing that. Mmm, that doesn't look good on you, have you seen my new broom?" The muttering and cursing carried on. Shanflax glanced down at the list of ingredients written for this citation in the propped-up book of shadows. She dipped a finger into the mixture, studied it and tasted it. "More mandrake, I think." Making herself useful by pulling the root out of the ground while Shiara was still muttering about sibling rivalry. The scream from the excised root was ear shattering. Shanflax wrapped a veil of her hair around it then dropped it into the pot with a plop. The screaming stopped immediately. The silence distracted Shiara from her distraction.

"I hope the mandrake didn't bite you."

Smirking slyly, Shanflax trotted closer to her. "You forget I'm mostly not of this plane. A little bit of poison and death is no problem to me." Shiara smiled and took Shanflax by the hands; her bronze skin, speckled with gold, shone and glittered, smooth and even, almost delicate to the touch.

"You know, Shanflax, I hate to admit it but I think I will need you." Shiara warmly smiled. "Thank you for appearing." Shanflax tenderly embraced the hands and warmly returned the compliment.

"I'm here to help, to assist I will, Shiara I am your servant."

"Don't talk wet, you either help or not." The sky had got noticeably purple with an orange glow just appearing in the far distance. Shiara braced herself. "Not long now. Shanflax, double time." She habitually put her arm down where Leonard was supposed to be. Grim determination flashed across her face, she had to reach the pinnacle of her objective. "Let's get this pantomime going. Could you get the cauldron up the hill while I nip up and prepare a circle? By the way you could call Ddraig Dŵr to give you a lift?" Shanflax looked on in awe at the funny little witch and smiled. Then she looked around. Ddraig Dŵr? Did she keep a dragon as a pet, if so, where was it hidden?

"Still the same old quirky Shiara," Shanflax thought them whistled as if calling a dog. A ripple of air and crumple of wings and Ddraig Dŵr appeared in the sky above. Magnificent and majestic. The shadow dweller couldn't help but be impressed.

8

Lord Witney

The bright daybreak sunshine drew long shadows. The intermittent trees spanned across the rolling hills where Worcestershire attaches to the gateway to Shropshire. A sharp spiked shadow looks like it pushes into the nurtured farmland, piercing the ploughed rows. The pointy silhouette belongs to a tall clock tower set into the hillside. Square in build, each wall has a large clock face. Ivory faces with large roman numerals in deepest black and great ebony hands designed to mark out the time clearly to the east, south, west and north.

All who gazed up at it are not all admirers, although it is a skilled and fine piece of engineering. The majority who keep time by it are the workers of the land that surrounds it. Not independent farmers or simple land workers. These men, women and children of all ages are in the employment of Lord Witney.

Lord Josher Witney was a lord by inheritance and not by valiant or heroic deed. His father had been a slave driver and unfortunately Lord Josher had learnt from one of the best. Due to an unfortunate twist of fate, Lord Witney senior passed the title to Lord Witney junior, all because of his own rules and as a stringent authoritarian. Witney senior had strict rules on what time housemaids could enter his chambers to wash and dress him. Under no circumstances could the maids enter the bath chamber between him entering at 7.30 a.m. and precisely 7.50 a.m. regardless of what sounds or rumpus was heard from outside. The lord had many strange habits which he kept to himself and his right-hand man, a self-styled sheriff called Brealue.

Seasoned skin, bearded and a good mass of dark hair framed his piercing ice blue eyes. The only clue of a harder existence in the past was a clear thick streak of grey/white hair from above his right eye all the way back across his head. He cut the frame of a strong action tarnished individual, practically dressed and always ready for action. The fateful morning Brealue was not present in the castle. Lord Witney had summoned the handmaidens to run and prepare his usual bath. At exactly 7.30 a.m. as the clock tower struck the maidens opened the ornate double doors to reveal the marble sunken bath with its gold faucets and cherubs pouring milk looking fluid into the reservoir of luxury. Lord Witney entered the marble bath chamber, disrobed, turning he closed the double doors himself for his instructed twenty minutes time alone.

Seven fifty-one had registered on the grandmother clock standing upright to the right of the bath chamber's ornate doors. One of the handmaidens, dressed in a black ankle-length dress with white semi-circular apron tied into a neat bow at the base of her spine, looked twice at the grand clock, physically double checking the time.

Click! 7.52. The handmaiden stood back with puzzlement, her face free of hair as it was drawn back severely into a bun on the crown of her head. Silence, total silence. The only thing to penetrate the quiet was the creak of her well-polished shoes as she inclined forward to place an ear to the door. No noise could be heard from behind the door. She was concentrating so much that she thought she heard a thump but soon realised it was her own heartbeat.

7.53. Most extraordinary. Two thoughts passed through her mind. Go and get someone else or go in and check on the master herself. She didn't relish the latter due to an incident she had heard about in the scullery. A maid entered the chamber unannounced. Officially she was moved on to work a more rural life on the fields. Unofficially, she only had the use of one arm and her face was so unrecognizable even her own family wouldn't accept her back. She toiled alone in a widow's shack away from everybody else making rag rugs. One day she felt so lonely. She took a rowing boat to the middle of the lake and just slipped quietly overboard. She was never seen again. Suddenly, the door at the bottom of the corridor burst open. The long pace of a military man comes striding up the corridor towards the maid. It was the figure of Brealue, marching, not breaking a step.

"Is our lord and master ready, girl?" The bellowing voice thundered down the hall. "I was summoned to be here at seven fifty-five," a dramatic nuance and the flourished arms added to his presence, "and here I am." The handmaiden took a polite step back as the self-styled sheriff had invaded her personal space. She glanced at the door then back to the fellow.

"He… he has not finished in the closet yet." Nervousness became evident on her face. "It is most peculiar. The master is normally so prompt." Brealue looked sternly at the girl.

"Why haven't you knocked? Aren't you worried about your master?" The girl spluttered and stuttered.

"We, well, er, yes, but we have strict instructions, not to enter under any circumstance. House rules. Always…" Brealue brushed the maiden aside and planted his ear firmly against the door. Nothing, not a sound. He rapped firmly on the japanned heavy wood door.

"Sir, this is Brealue." His voice loud and clear. "Are you all right in there, sir?" They were met with a deafening silence. The girl started to shrink away, feeling a dreadful fear growing in her belly. She stepped backwards; a squelch sounded from where she trod. Both Brealue and the maid examined the carpet below them. To their horror they quickly realised that it was sodden. The water had soaked from underneath the door. Acting quickly and by instinct the sheriff stepped back, held a hand up to move the maid out of the way and kicked at the lock of the doors. The sole of his well-heeled riding boots thundered against aged oak. The door creaked under the attack but held firm. Bolstering his effort he took a further step back and really went for it with his whole body. The door creaked but held fast. Brealue took in a good lungful of air and launched a two-footed flying kick aimed towards the middle of the doors. The lock gave way with a screech of metal on iron. The left door unhinged itself from its stay, the right simply swung inwards. The maid closed her eyes. Trying to shield her face in case the master came flying out, riding crop in hand, flailing at her face.

Brealue walked into the room, leather boots squelching on the carpet. The room looked empty. Nobody was in the chamber. The only movement was a trickle of water coming from the edge of the bath, the bath water ran over a sculpture of the cherub onto the floor. Brealue glanced around the bathroom and made his way towards the sumptuous marble bathtub. It was full to the brim and still as a mill pond. Investigating further he noticed the dark shadowed shape of a body at the bottom of the bath. He crept closer and peered over and into the tub. A sudden movement in the depth of the water made him start. The surprise made the girl sharply jump back against the wall. Both of her hands raced to cover her mouth and stifle a scream.

A tiny green head the size of a tomato with opaque black eyes broke the still surface. Ripples radiated outwards from it in rings. Both of the humans in the bathroom were taken aback. Brealue almost stumbled backwards over a laundry basket. The maid recognized the creature.

"Grindylow!" A hand fell from her mouth. "It's a grindylow." Brealue looked astonished at the green creature then back towards the girl. "Oh no! Wait! They normally come in..." The water erupted, interrupting the girl's sentence. Two more grindylows burst from the water. "Threes."

The grindylows stood on two legs, humanoid in shape but about the same height as a cat. Their long fingers and toes have suckers at the end of each digit, frog-like. They made a strange squeal as they turned and fled through the small crack in the bathroom window frame. The last one twisted its disturbing head around, flashed its demonic eyes and gave an evil grin before squealing and slipping through the window. Once the shock of seeing the creatures subsided, Brealue sprinted to the overflowed bath and delved his arm into the water. He struggled to pull the remains of Lord Witney. Both of his palms slippery with suds and lather, he struggled to hold the corpse steady. The face of the lord was bloated and wide-eyed. The expression was quite comical in a morbid sort of way, a rigor toothy grin.

"My dear, what were those things?" He rested one hand under the back of the head, holding the face out of the water.

"They were grindylows. My mother used to warn me about them." She had come nearer now as if not afraid of the master anymore. "They are water daemons and normally are only found in rivers, ponds and lakes. Grindylows have long fingers that drag children into the deep if they misbehave. They don't normally go after grown men." The girl had become wide-eyed and quite excited. "I wonder who or what sent them?" She was in full swing now, brain working overtime. Looking out of the window a thought struck the maid. "I've got it!"

"Who? What could have sent them?" Brealue had started to be drawn into the girl's stories.

"Maybe it was a rusalka," she pondered.

"A rusalka? What in my mad aunt's name is a rusalka?" The girl settled on the side of the bath now, twirling her fingers playfully in the water.

"A rusalka is thought to be the soul of a young woman who has died prematurely due to suicide or murder within water. They carry on in this world but only as a spirit until their death is avenged." Brealue visibly shuddered.

"Well, who could put such a curse on this honourable gentleman?" It was the girl's time to bristle.

"Honourable! Gentleman! Don't make me laugh, he was and will always be known as a monster." Brealue was taken aback. "He beat my predecessor so badly that her own family didn't recognized her. In all her woe, she took her own life in the lake." Trembling with passion she continued, "I hope and pray that her tortured soul can rest now." The maid turned and looked out of the window onto the nearby lake. "Please rest, dear Abather, rest now, the monsters gone." A thunderclap and a rapid flash of lightning sounded in the distance. Brealue, shocked and feeling misled stared misty-eyed upon the girl.

"What is your name, child?" The worlds were gentle and hushed in their delivery.

"May, short for Maydle, sir." May gave him a shy smile.

"May, my dear, will you leave this pit of deception with me, please. I cannot associate myself with this," with disgust he slips the dead lord's head out of his hand and watches it sink once more into the water, "this fiend." Brealue looks up earnestly at the young maid. "Please come with me. We shall start elsewhere. I have a cousin who is a candle maker in Cleobury Mortimer. Will you join me?" His hands were outstretched, she looked at him quizzically. He dropped to one knee, the look of pleading on his face. Her heart melted as her eyes met and sank into his.

"I have no family, I have no ties or friends and as of now, I have no employment. Of course I will come with you. It will be an adventure."

Brealue rose to his feet grinning. "It's hardly an adventure."

May fell into his arms and placed her head onto his chest. "My dear Brealue, it is for me."

Later that day Josher Witney came back to the manor to find his head maid and sheriff gone. His father lay drowned in the bath. Not wanting the crown or authorities snooping around the estate, the new Lord Witney registered the death of his father as drunkenness in the bath. The old Lord Witney didn't die in spirit though. Lord Witney Jnr carried forward with his father's template of high profit-low expenditure. He didn't count human beings as valuable in his business; to him they were expendable, easily replaced. So, there was Lord

Josher Witney Jnr, lord of all he surveyed, master of the manor and king of his own kingdom. He presided alone in his court, surrounded by his wealth and looking down on the poor. He stared out of the ornate window over the rolling fields, alone. Hands behind his back, eyes cold and unfeeling.

9

The Big Bang

Shiara was making her way up the incline that would eventually lead to the summit of Titterstone Clee, the topmost point above the village of Cleehill, multi-coloured bag strapped across her back and staff in hand. Concentration and determination locked into her features she never broke pace, carving a determined path through terrain over heather and rocks. Darkness briefly put her into shadow. Shiara noticed the outline of Ddraig Dŵr passing overhead, soaring majestically towards the top of the hill. She could just make out the outline of the cauldron, Pair Dadeni and the silhouette of a figure on the nape of the dragon's neck, Shanflax. "Lazy sod!" exclaimed the wise one; with a smile and a wave she doubled her pace. The dragon continued to circle until Shiara had made it to the zenith. Trotting now, she motioned and pointed to the area that she wanted them to land.

Standing in the middle of a flat area she unloaded her bag and quickly surveyed the patch of land. Grabbing her staff and muttering some words she held it firmly in both hands and drove it into the ground. Walking a circle she never opened her eyes or looked where she was going, but swift and perfect the scoured circle became. Raising her face to the sky she smiles and opens her eyes, taking in all the splendour of the morning sky. Ddraig Dŵr and Shanflax hovered until she beckoned them down to the circle. Playfully the dragon swoops down but pulls up, hovering gracefully just above the circle. Grasping the bottom legs of the cauldron she tips about a third of the mixture into the middle of the circle. Shanflax slides down the dragon's back, off the tail and smoothly onto the ground. The dragon senses the next part of the plan so hovers up with cauldron still in her grasp. The shadow dweller, still in her more solid form, slithers up next to Shiara. "All going to plan, my beautiful one?" The hushed tone oozed from Shanflax even though they were alone. "What is it you want me to do?" Shiara turns to her side, their faces very close.

"I want you to do the most important part of this plan." Shiara paused with a look of total earnestness. "I want you to return to your shadow state and when you get the chance I want you to get hold of and protect Leonard." She tilted her neck as if listening for the giant. "Also can you hold my bag?" Smiling Shiara quickly produced two stones from her bag, one dark stone which looked almost glittery, as if a thousand galaxies were trapped inside. The other was an orange and black striped stone known as a tiger's eye. Once more she dug into the shoulder bag and yielded a pretty drawstring bag made from brushed velvet, purple in colour. Shanflax gratefully took the shoulder bag and shimmered as if caught inside a mist. Licking blue flames emitted from her feet and soon engulfed her body, returning her to her shadow form. The shadow slinked away to the shade of a rock in which she was totally camouflaged. Looking up Shiara noticed that Ddraig Dŵr was still hovering, cauldron in claw.

"I'm sorry my darling, I almost forgot you." She walked thirty-three paces and drove the staff into the ground again. This was a bigger circle but still perfectly round. Shiara completed her task with method and grace. Beckoning the dragon down for the second time, Shiara held the legs of the cauldron and poured the remainder of the concoction into the centre of the larger circle. Fizzing and bubbling, the mixture soaked into the ground. "Thank you, dear friend." Ddraig Dŵr lowers his head to meet Shiara's and they nuzzle and embrace each other. "Now be off with you and could you drop the cauldron off at home, please," the dragon nods, rubbing his head against her again, "that's a good boy." Ddraig Dŵr unfurls mighty wings and takes off into the air with the grace and nimbleness of an eagle. Shiara watches the mighty beast glide and coast down the hill, cauldron clasped in the front claw.

The dragon was soaring towards Cleobury when her eye catches a large form ambling up the hill. The dragon in a fit of mischief nosedived towards the puffing and wheezing figure. He spurted out some hot water from his nostrils, covering the giant. Bradnock roared and tried to swat the dragon. Uprooting a nearby oak tree in anger, the giant took a swing for the dragon with the tree. A simple flick of the tail and the dragon had dodged the lumbering hulk, happily flapping away into the distance. The giant cursed and wiped the sweat from his clammy brow and neck with a check patterned handkerchief the size of a bed sheet. Bradnock carried on trudging up the incline, pulling the branches and peeling the bark off the oak to make the trunk more streamlined and smooth. Shiara watched the little exchange with amusement. She skipped back to the first smaller circle, producing the dark stone with the stardust trapped in it. She held it tight in her left hand, muttering some wondrous words;

May the stars in this stone,
Fly high but not alone,
Sparkle now with truth and might, Give this circle power, Grow and make right.

Casting the stone into the centre immediately caused a stir in the earth. A twist of green sprouted up, then around the stone a vine grew; cupping the stone like a prize the greenery engorged upwards, flourishing as it went, developing into a thick stem the width of a small tree. The stone also enlarged as the vine matured, inflated by the stars within its unfathomable surface, as if the mini universe within was trying to get out. This testament to nature's power grew and grew until it was the height of a large apple tree with an enormous black glittery orb sitting on the top, nurtured and being held by the nest of vines.

"What's happenin' here?" a booming voice announced, echoing into the distance like rolling thunder.

10
Top of the World

Bradnock had finally reached the pinnacle of the summit. Beads of sweat trickled down his forehead, got caught in his mono-brow, distributing the droplets either side of his face, saving his eyes from the sting of salty perspiration. His lower lip drooped low after the last words were literally spat out, a gobbet of spittle hanging, swinging in the breeze. He looked down at Shiara with some malice, leaning forward on his newly fashioned club made out of the oak tree.

"Well hello, little witch," bits of saliva spluttered out, "what have you been busy doing?" Shiara reflected back his malice with serenity and calm. Breaking from the stare, she opened her arms wide and looked around the three-hundred-and-sixty-degree view. The landscape panorama overlooks thirteen counties; gentle, rolling, multicolour hills, undulating far into the distance, creating an uneven horizon. "Nice of you to join me on this marvellously beautiful morning," Shiara smiled. "How did you sleep?" The giant leant forward on his oak club, his weight making it creak.

"Okay, little sorceress, enough of the chit chat. How are you going to make me king of this land?" Shiara looked at him curiously, and then let her smile return to her face. "To be a king you would have to be born a noble and I'll bet my last swede you are not posh." The giant looked blank, not registering the sly insult. "I'm going to make you a hero." The giant straightened up, seeming to like that idea. "Firstly, where is Leonard?" A stern look crossed Shiara's face, eyes fixed on Bradnock. "No worries, little one. It is here." Reaching around into a satchel made from worn-out rags, the huge hand produced the lynx being held by the scruff of its neck. Shiara held her anger back and grasped her staff tightly. "His name is Leonard and he is a lynx, now put him down gently," she growled through gritted teeth. The giant lowered the big cat to the floor behind him, barring the cat's way with his foot. The lynx's ears pricked up, eyes widened and licked his lips as if trying to taste the air. Shiara stepped forward but Bradnock waved an index finger and gave out an audible tut.

"Oh no tiny lady, it stays behind me until your spell is done." Shiara leant on her staff and sagged, looking dejected, but secretly she was overjoyed at the giant's choice as Bradnock didn't notice the stirring in the shadows. From the rock behind Bradnock the shadow lengthened. Looking like an elongated hand the shadow shrouded the lynx and retracted into the shadow of the rock. Shiara raised her head, satisfied that her familiar was safe for now.

The wise woman looked up at the glistening ball on top of the sturdy erect stem. "Right Bradnock, you have to win the trust of the villagers and townsfolk alike. So, you need to do as I ask." The giant tried to look menacing but the prospect of becoming a mighty, respected ruler of his own land was too good to pass by.

"Okey dokey, what do we need to do?"

The slight childishness in the giant's manner amused Shiara, how something so big could seem quite innocent. Bradnock may have sensed this as he puffed out his chest and drew himself up to his full height. "Tell me my task and I will show you a chief." Shiara found it hard to stifle a titter because of this show of mock masculinity.

"We shall go for a show of strength, puzzle solving and precision." She stroked her chin. "It is not going to be easy."

"Just tell me my task, you old hag," Bradnock stiffened and bellowed.

"Okay, okay, hold your horses, big boy. What you need to do is to get this beautiful stone over the clock tower, over there." Bradnock strained his eyes and saw the pointed roof of the grand clock, looked back at the witch then back at the tower.

"Over the top, you say?"

"Yes, over the top, but you cannot touch the stone with your hands or it will explode. You cannot enter the circle or the stone and vine will wither and return to the ground." The giant was a bit perplexed and leant on his club. The creak of the wood appeared to give him an idea.

"I know what to do." The cocksure persona had returned. "Stand back. This is going to be impressive."

Hoisting the club up and over his right shoulder, Bradnock took a few paces backwards as if measuring the distance. Then, with an almighty turn of power, the goliath swung the stripped tree in an arc, swinging and turning full circle. On the second full turn the wide trunk of the club connected with the glittering black orb. A shower of sparks emitted from the struck globe as the improvised bat made contact. Rocketing off like a meteor, the engorged stone hurtled through the blue sky towards the clock tower in the distance. Bradnock stumbled backwards and ended up down on one knee following the force from the blow. Shiara opened her eyes to see the wonderful fizzing rainbow colours the stone left behind as it flew like a comet. The stone narrowly missed the roof, and went past it.

"I DID IT!" There was an element of disbelief to the giant's tone of voice. Then he realised. "I did it." He turned to Shiara, who was still watching the progress of the stone with some interest. She raised her hand and listened intently. An amazing plume of purple smoke appeared in the distance behind the ridge of the tower. A rumble followed by an echoed explosion. The purple mist was replaced by black smoke.

11

Run Lord Run

What happened to that magic ball? What was the puff of purple mist? What caused the fire and explosion? What did the orb hit? Over the top of the clock tower the bloated stone flew. A trail of glitter and multicolour sparks glistened in its tail. It shot past the clock tower roof and over the hill. There stood Witney Court, proud and grand with its golden dome resplendent and visible for miles around. The grand entrance did not expect what was coming. The only occupant of the house that morning didn't notice the gorgeous meteor that was hurtling towards the mock roman pillars that stood at the front.

The lord was admiring his profile in the ostentatious, gilt-framed mirror that dominated the lavender-tinted, luxuriant room. He was just adjusting his white bouffant wig when the ground shook for the first time. A look of terror invaded the powder-coated, made-up face of the noble. The wig tilted to a slanted angle as he tried to gather up his flowing silk skirts. In the panic the wig fell. The flustered man's bald pate of a scalp, quite pink in contrast to the white china clay make-up, was exposed. Darting to the doors and flinging them open he ran to the balustrade. Leaning over the handrail the lord was alarmed by what he saw.

The shimmering fireball burst into the lower floor of the grand house. Sparks flicked outwards towards every surface it passed. Little iridescent embers tumbled into the sumptuous carpets, starting a little trail of fire. The ball of fire appeared to have a mind of its own. It started weaving between the pillars.

Then, it seemed to have found its prey. The fiery orb arced around and hurtled for the stairs. The lord suddenly became conscious of its obvious intention. Dropping his skirts and unclasping the braces, the much-undignified lord hurried out of his bizarre attire and sprinted off down the art-laden corridor. The comet coasted up the stairwell, leaving a blazing path of fire, and continued towards its target, the one and only Lord Witney Jnr. Free from the straps and bondage of his garments the startled noble was fleeing in his white cotton underwear. Unfortunately his all in one had unbuttoned at the back, exposing his skinny pink bum. As the ball drew closer to him the heat could be felt particularly well in the derrière region. The hairless-headed man raced down the hallways being constantly chased by the fantastic sphere. The pair dashed, raced and hurtled through the passageways and alcoves. The flaming ball looked like it was attached to the fleeing white figure by a length of string because it was so precise in its pursuit.

Each room that the lord hurtled through the ball followed, igniting small fires as it went. Hounded by the ball from hell, the man was frightened out of his wits. The only way out appeared like a white vision of light in front of him. The arched doors of the brilliant white conservatory were open as if welcoming him to safety. The lord doubled his efforts and planned to make a jump to safety out of the exit doors.

Creating a small amount of space between the meteor and himself, the lord barrelled through the first set of doors. Flinging his arms out wide, he managed to catch the edge of the doors and swing them shut. Boom! The explosion seemed to push him forward faster. The ball had shattered the doors and looked a slight bit smaller. It also lost some momentum skipping along the surface, causing puffs of orange, purple, yellow as it impacted on the ground. Edged on by his minor victory, Witney headed towards the outer double doors at full pelt. The flame ball had lost some more energy and had started to roll across the floral terrain of the hothouse. Sparks and shattered shards of kindles flew off from the rolling ball, igniting orange trees and wooded plants and creating enchanting plumes of multi-coloured smoke. Witney made the mistake of looking over his shoulder; alarm set in as he saw that the ball was still speeding towards him. He dug his toes in and tore towards the waiting exit. The glowing ball was almost trapping his heels as he thundered through the door and plunged through the air of the bright spring morning sunlight.

The coolness and thinness of the daybreak air whistled through the flaps and gaps of his tattered nightwear. It was not much of a drop but the fall felt like time was running backwards. Plummeting towards the ground another blast exploded inside the conservatory, blowing the windows outwards. The flying lord was showered with razor sharp shards of glass. The earth cushioned the not so graceful nobleman, as he crumpled into a rose bush head first.

In that prone position the lord shuffled, moved to the left and collapsed. Turning onto his back he looked back towards the house, pupils darting around the area in fear and foreboding as the lord took in the sight of the still standing grandiose house. At the exact moment it took for the noble to breathe out, it collapsed. Seemingly from the back, the rumble carried through and pushed an enormous cloud of smoke with it. Like a dragon breathing out fire, the manor exhaled fire, brimstone and a big belch of grey/black smoke. It pushed the lord backward, bathed with heat, solar and biomass into the grass. Now covered in the grey soot, the flattened lord was camouflaged against the ground. The only thing that differentiated him from the greyness was the pink wetness that had started to leak from his eyes. His red maw of a mouth opened as the cry of loss poured from the stricken noble.

12

Huffs and Puffs

Trying to regain some composure the giant first leant on his club then got up onto one knee. Using his almighty hand to push up from the ground, his unsteadiness reminded Shiara of an overgrown toddler trying to stand. The ascent was not the most graceful but he did it.

"Did I do it?" rubbing his forehead and blinking into the distance, the goliath asked. Shiara also looked into the distance, observing a little spiral of smoke rising from the area of the house of Lord Witney Jnr.

"I think you might have done part one." Hands on her hips she faced Bradnock. "Well done." The giant beamed like a pampered child; it took a second to register.

"PART ONE?" The bellow seemed to shake the hill they stood on. "WHAT DO YOU MEAN? PART ONE?" Shiara looked innocently into the eyes of Bradnock. "I mean, well done young man," she batted her long eyelashes, "part one done, that means you only have part two to do."

"PART TWO?" Bradnock was starting to get confused. "You said nothing about it being more than one task."

"I never said it was only going to be one task. Anyway you are well on the way to becoming the people's hero. Do you want to carry on?" The deep endless pools of loveliness of Shiara's eyes bewitched Bradnock. He had to shake himself out of the mesmerizing stare.

"Well, what do I have to do in part two, then?" Bradnock was now full of confidence, ready for anything. Shiara sauntered up to the next prepared circle and hovered by its perimeter.

"Much the same really, but you have only got to get this orb into the devil's punchbowl at Clows Top."

"Oh. Okay, that's easy." Bradnock was being very self-assured now, striding purposely up to where the wise woman stood.

"Where is the ball?"

"Whoa, there, big boy," her hand rose to slow the buoyant giant, "this one will be a touch larger." The giant was taking practice swings, bombastically.

"No problem little lady, I'll do it whatever the size." Shiara looked quizzically at him then composed herself at the circle's edge. "So mote it be." She tossed the tiger's eye stone into the dead centre of the circle with a flick of her thumb. The chosen words were uttered;

"May this offering flourish,
Root, feed and sprout,
As above,
So below,
Through this stone,
Please grow."

The earth in the middle of the circle moved into a swirl shape, not unlike the middle of a conch shell. The grooves filled with water and carried on filling until the entire circle was fingernail deep with crystal clear water. The circle of water settled so it was still and reflected the azure blue sky. Its mirror-like surface, perfect in its reflection and tranquillity, looked like a pool of quicksilver. It looked like it was not of this world. Then something started to move from inside of the pool. It looked like a small insect, similar to a water boatman, was making its way inward from the edge to the centre in a perfect spiral. Bradnock was transfixed on the pattern it created.

The tiny creature was a youngling of Ceffyl Dŵr, a magical water horse that had a good and bad reputation. In north Wales, adult Ceffyl Dŵrs are known to leap out of the water to trample and kill people who are lost. It is not known whether they do this on purpose or by mistake. They entice the unwary traveller to ride them. Flying into the air, the Ceffyl Dŵr evaporates, dropping the unfortunate rider to their death. In south Wales they are known as cheeky pests. Appearing as winged horses and tempting travellers with quick transportation but then disappearing. Shiara had befriended an infant Ceffyl Dŵr near mid Wales. It had no parents or guardians so she took the little animal in to make sure it was safe. Now the little water horse was reaching maturity, Shiara knew she would have to let him go so, he could grow. Before release, Shiara persuaded the water horse to perform this spell, promising to take it to the mountain pass in Snowdon, north Wales, where it could carry out its rowdy teenage years before withdrawing to south Wales for a sedate retirement. A human year is equal to seventy years to a Ceffyl Dŵr so sadly in just over a year's time this water horse will have died of old age. That is if he makes it that far, pesky and reckless as they can be. Shiara would protect this little water horse the best she could, as this fifteen-minute spell took up an entire day in his time scale. For this Shiara was very grateful.

The tiny Ceffyl Dŵr was spiralling inwards and then outwards, making what became an intricate figure of eight that produced a miniature whirlpool in the centre. The water started to look sculptured, with the Ceffyl Dŵr darting this way and that, creating an amazingly sophisticated pattern. The centre was now a good four feet high, looking like an ornate clear crystal vase. A gust of wind blew Shiara's hair out of her face as she concentrated, arms out wide. The air only lightly ruffled Bradnock's fringe but the look of bafflement was clear on his face. The squall had a wonderful earthy smell about it with a hint of marigold and gorse. Shiara held out her left hand, flat palm up, as her right was rummaging in her bag that was slung across her chest. Ceffyl Dŵr finished a neat pirouette, spun in the air, landing deftly onto the waiting hand on all four hooves. The created inverted whirlpool of water continued as Shiara produced a rag-wrapped branch from her seemingly bottomless bag.

"With the spirit of the North,
Earth does sow,
To the West,
Waters flow,
With the spirit of East,
Air will roll,
Take Fire from the South,
This plant will grow."

The ragged branch in her right-hand burst into flames. Even Bradnock felt the power of this spell and wise woman. He had a small doubt in the back of his self-possessed mind that he may have underestimated this little lady. She held the flaming torch forward into the funnel of the water, continuing to mutter the chosen words. The updraft of marigold and gorse caused the flame to flurry for a while then it started a flare-up within the funnel. A wave of brilliant blue flame grew outwards like a bulb. Shiara withdrew the torch which was spent now and just shouldered. Her eyes were alive and alight with the magnificent flame in front of her. The little eyes of Ceffyl Dŵr appeared to be engrossed in the power of the furnace. Only Bradnock looked slightly fearful and wondering what he had let himself in for.

While Shiara, Bradnock and the Ceffyl Dŵr were transfixed on the developing spell the shadow beside the rock where Leonard the lynx was tethered shifted. The shifting darkness embraced the big cat, concealing it totally. Not a sound was heard.

The flourishing flame had started changing colours now. From bright blue, aquamarine, to sea green the flame continued to change into new and wonderful iridescent colours. The kaleidoscope of shimmering colours took the form of an irregular ball on top of a crystal base. The water funnel base had hardened off now but seemed to keep an aquiline structure. It still looked like running water but was solid as rock. It had also grown in height. It was as tall as the market hall in the village, about the same height as Bradnock's shoulder. Shiara managed to peel her eyes away from her handiwork and looked down at the tiny water horse in her left hand. "Thank you, cariad." The Ceffyl Dŵr flicked its front two hooves up in enjoyment. Knowing that the giant would still be awestruck by the enormous psychedelic plant bulb, Shiara sneaked over to the shady area where Leonard was tied up. He wasn't there. Shiara spun around in panic, where the hell was he? "It's ok, sister dear. I've got your familiar safe." The coldness of the speech would give the shivers to anyone.

"Shanflax, is that you?" Leonard's head appeared as if floating in mid-air. The shadow dweller was shielding the lynx and playing tricks. "Oh, there you are, Leo." The smile of love was real and deep. "Shanflax, can you keep these two safe and concealed, please?" She passed the water horse into the shadow. "Make sure they are un-tied in case we need to make a quick getaway." The shadow shifted.

"Are you not confident with your own plan?" A slightly mocking tone emanated from the shadow dweller. Shiara, for the first time, looked a bit nervous but she rallied. "Of course I am." She bit her lip, betraying her nervousness.

13

Colours Fly and Catherine Wheel

Clee Hill at its peak is majestic. During the current sunrise the view was breathtaking. Clear light and golden rays enriched the azure blue sky that got deeper and more vivid the higher Shiara looked into the sky. Thirteen counties can be seen from the summit and the open sky looked and felt vast. It felt like they were standing on top of the world. Now there was a new object that would become a landmark on the hill.

Before the unlikely pair of the giant and Shiara stood a huge globular sphere, beautiful in its irregularity and wonderfully vibrant with varied patterns. Dashes of primary colours at the base and eddies of intermixed clashing pigment built up into twizzles of vivacious day-glo hues. It looked alive with pulsating and flamboyant shades, garish yet matching, in its uniform disarray. A dazzling orb sat on top of the fine-looking, almost exquisite stalk, which looked like a delicate vase of cut crystal. A virtuoso in glass. Rainbow colours were being cast into the grass from the sunrays penetrating the stalk and causing a prism effect. The green was lost in the grass but the red and blue highlighted and danced within the blades like dainty faerie folk searching out the dark to make light again.

Bradnock was taken aback by the other-worldly splendour of the object, which stood erect against the magnificence of the sunrise. The spectacle of this natural event, coupled with the presentation of a delightful sculpture created by magic, touched a well-hidden emotion within the giant. It had been a long time since an object of loveliness had moved him. The reason he became nocturnal and the cause of his loneliness came back to him in a wave of sentiment.

Shiara noticed the contemplative expression on Bradnock's face. Her mindreading skills were rusty but she could see that something was unsettling the giant. Even though giants could be ruthless, single-minded, selfish, greedy and bigoted there seemed to be a spark of morality within Bradnock at this particular moment. She decided on an open question, so as not to pressure Bradnock into opening his heart, that's if he had one.

"It is a delightful daybreak." Her wide smile came with a delicate chuckle. "Makes you feel glad to be alive." Her hands were settled on hips, her breast heaved as she took deep lungful of air. It was as if she was trying to ventilate her whole body with the sunny anther. Bradnock looked down at her through his mismatched eyes, the misty one looked a little hazier. His mind seemed to be in a different place, not focused. Absent screams from the past crept up on him like a spectra.

14

Bradnock's Secret

Rain poured down over the vast landlocked lake. It was so wide it could be classed as a loch. Heavy drops caused the surface of the water to dance and undulate. Small waves broke onto the rock slate shore. This was Llyn Cwm-y-ffynnon, a lake below the summit of Moel Berfedd in Cwmffynnon, a wonderfully beautiful clear area of Snowdon, Wales, not far from the legendary town of Beddgelert.

The young giant cut a solitary figure; sitting on a felled yew tree he looked out over the rippling surface of the shimmering lake. Between two large hands, he delicately held a flute. A delicate greenish glow radiated from it. The flute looked ethereal, not of this world. It seemed to pulsate; when the breeze blew over the holes on the fragile shaft, haunting notes came from it. The sound was calm and haunting, almost like an earthly angel singing notes and melodies, no words. Such a wondrous resonance carried across the scenic lake, echoing off the peaks and valleys. The melody reverberated in the valley. The fresh-faced young Bradnock was searching for something. Meticulously scanning the dancing surface with his emerald eyes, crystal clear and keen, he could pinpoint the smallest movement in the lake. The unruly mop of hair was plastered down onto his forehead due to the rain. The ruffled eyebrow did its job perfectly, keeping the water from running into his eyes.

Bradnock was playing the magic flute of the mermaids. The flute was legendary and was known by the name

Mynephort. It was given to Bradnock's grandmother by a mermaid who had got stuck inside of the blowhole in Boscastle Harbor, Cornwall. The mermaid was trying to hide from an amorous sailor who had been spying on her sunbathing. When the sailor tried to make advances, the mermaid dived into the harbor and hid in a cave. Unfortunately, she had mistimed the hiding place and the tide came in quicker than she had expected. Suddenly she was left with two choices. Stay in the cave and get beaten senseless by the tide's current pouring into the blowhole, or chance swimming out of the submerged cave right into the net of the lustful sailor. The mermaid opted for the latter, trying for the open sea. In one impressive dive she swam deep and swiftly along the dark tunnel. It seemed much further in the dark murky water. Her breath was running out. Above her, like a glass ceiling, the mermaid saw the surface of the sea and could not see any net or trap. As her statuesque head and shoulders broke the surface, the mermaid glanced at the harbor wall. There, standing impressively monumental, was a female giant, legs astride the mouth of the harbor that leads to the village of Boscastle. Taken aback by the enormity of the giant at first, the mermaid didn't notice what was dangling from the giant's hand. The sailor was being held by the scruff of the neck like a naughty cat. The giant was telling him off, shaking him like a rag doll. Neona, the mermaid, made her way to the harbor wall and unbuckled the flute from her belt and placed it onto the giant's foot. Patting the great toe and blowing a kiss, the mermaid pitched forward and swam away free.

Radsock, the giant, knew that some mermaids were mute and Neona must have been one of them. Almost like disposing of some rubbish, Radsock tossed the sailor to one side. Luckily for him he landed unconscious in the boughs of a tree. The giant kept the flute safe for many summers until she gave it to her grandson Bradnock on his fifth birthday.

Bradnock had treasured the flute and it never left his side. This was the time, thought Bradnock, the flute and he would show his brothers his strength. He would prove that he was a proper mature giant by getting one of the most dangerous creatures around.

An indefinable shape broke the surface of the water to the right of the teenage giant. Eyes like an eagle and reactions equal to a cobra, Bradnock was on his feet and down to the shore as quick as a flash. The water broke again, a spray of water shot into the air. Suddenly, a fork-shaped tail aggressively broke the surface of the water, creating huge waves. The main body of the beast burst through the surface of water, its grotesque head pivoting on a very stout neck. It looked like an oversized beaver with a cruel, almost reptilian, face. Bradnock quickly grabbed and pulled at the thick rope that was half-hidden in the shale of the shore. The sloppy, worn rope was connected to an ancient net that the creature had been lured into. Struggling to keep hold of the slippery rope, Bradnock hauled with all of his might. The soles of his massive brown leather boots dug into the stony shore, causing them to submerge slightly as he grappled with the rope. With the weight of purpose and grit singing in his brain, Bradnock was determined to capture this creature even if it killed him.

The Afanc that Bradnock had just bagged was originally from the Bearded Lake, Llyn Barfog. The Afanc was known to cause floods and drown passers-by. When the people of Llyn Barfog wanted to rid themselves of the Afanc they set a trap.

The singing voice of a virgin lady is the only known way to attract the monster ashore. The fair maiden sat and sang all day but at night the brute slithered ashore and fell asleep on her lap. While the creature slumbered, the lady stroked and lullabied the beast. Twenty villagers waited. Once they were sure the beast was asleep they took a chance. The beast was chained down as best as they could. The monstrosity awoke and thrashed about so violently that it killed the poor singing female. However, after a while the chains held fast and the beast became fatigued. It was then safely captured. The whole town dragged the Afanc away to Lake Cwm Ffynnon, where it now finds itself caught up in the net of Bradnock.

Strain and sweat were apparent on the giant's face as he tried with all his might to haul the creature out of the water. It was near him now. Water was being showered everywhere in great torrents. Great surges of lake water slammed into the young giant. Hand over hand Bradnock kept on pulling, determination taking over. Pure willpower dulling the pain he felt in his arms and shoulders. Being half drowned did not help the task. The creature was getting nearer. The smell of silt and rotted fish filled his nostrils, slime covered his hands but his grip remained firm. As more of the beast was exposed, Bradnock could understand why it was so feared. The flesh was uneven and pitted, leather-like on the surface but inside the round pits were tufts of grey fur. Rolls of bloated soft tissue, flabby and blubbery, made up its main body, webbed, duck-like flippers sticking out of each corner. The head was angular and had a reptilian evilness about it. The tail was the most lethal. Three pronged and sturdy, the tail possessed a range that could extend far beyond its own body length.

As quick as lightning and as sleek as a snake, the tail slashed and struck the giant in the face. The first prong scraped his scalp, causing him to duck. The second prong met his lower lip, stinging it like a hornet; the swelling was immediate as the poison was injected. Bradnock didn't feel the third prong, it was aimed with impeccable intention. The giant felt only a slight pressure above his right eye. As he did not feel any pain he continued pushing forward. The prong simply pierced itself underneath a couple of layers of the iris and slid. Like peeling an orange, the sight in the giant's eye was taken, quick, simple, effective. Bradnock fell. The giant dropped to his knees, his right hand to his face, the pain taking over. Releasing the soaking rope, his left hand joined its sibling over his swollen disjointed aspect.

The wet rope splashed down and submerged back into the lake. A cascade of white water covered the floored junior giant as he sat back onto his haunches, bent double, whining as he caressed his face. The Afanc felt the relaxed grip on the rope net and made its getaway, taking the net and rope with it. Bradnock just sat there dazed and confused. The grotesque beast seemed to rise up in the water; with its sinister eyes it looked at what damage it had done to the giant. Apparently not satisfied with its reprise, the Afanc pushed and heaved the weapon of a tail and bloated body to create an enormous wave. The wall of water rushed towards the incapacitated Bradnock, knocking him backwards and flat on his back. The giant was out cold after thumping his head on the slated shore. Once the mini tsunami had subsided, the Afanc surveyed the scene once more. Cruel eyes rolled as its distended form floated towards the prone figure on the shoreline. The calculations going on in the diabolical mind were conniving. Then with an unexpected turn, the Afanc swung around and swam away, leaving an arrow shaped bow in the water behind.

Maybe it was something it saw in the trees or it may have gauged that Bradnock was too big to digest at this present time. It was gone. With that, Bradnock would live to fight another day. The problem for the unconscious teen giant was not the monster that he had just encountered. It was the two very large hobnail boots that were standing beside his head. Unaware and comatose, Bradnock didn't feel the massive shovel-like hand grip his shoulders and pick him up like a rag doll.

"Wakey wakey, twinkle toes," boomed the gravel-laden tone. "Time to make you really suffer."

15

Wake Up Sleepy Head

Bradnock's head swam with fresh nightmares and the strange feeling of not knowing where he was. The last he remembered was being soaking wet and a sharp pain in his head. No, an excruciating pain that was around his head and in his eye. His eye! His massive hand shot up and felt where the eye was supposed to be; in its place was material of some sort. Padded material, a rough outer bit, and the inner felt like it was soothing his eye. Putting his arm back beside himself, Bradnock used his one remaining one eye to look and try and get his bearings on where he was.

The light was poor and he could only make out shadows dancing on the rough beamed ceiling, made by the flickering candles. Then to the left he noticed and recognized an enormous room-filling scythe.

"Oh, that's torn it. I'm in trouble now!"

The dangerous, lethal-looking instrument was very well cared for. The curved half-moon blade glinted with precise polishing. The edge looked sharp and as deadly as any razor edge could. The ornate and handsomely carved stem held the knife blade firmly and precisely. Entwined carving of poison ivy leaf and snakes meandered around the thick sturdy stem till it met with the plain but highly polished handle. Polished with use and handling. Bradnock recognized the implement and realised where he was. He was home, lying on the kitchen table.

His heart sank because he couldn't remember anything since pulling at his net. Therefore, it could only mean two things. One, he was successful in catching the Afanc or two, he had failed miserably and he was injured and on the kitchen table. Maybe he had died and he was lying in state on the table. His soul was still in his body waiting for the scores of mourners to file through and pay their respects. Bradnock closed his eye, trying to look serene and noble.

"Are you awake yet?" The rumble of a voice clattered from a distance then burst into the room. "Wake up, you pathetic boil on an otter's arse." Bradnock did not move. It may have been because of fright or if he ignored the voice it might go away.

"Right, that's it." The expression of the voice changed from annoyance to fury. There was a flurry of activity, clattering of pots and pans. Then Bradnock felt himself being pushed off the wooden table. As he flew, in the split second between the table and the ground, Bradnock enjoyed the feeling of weightlessness. The cast iron cooker made contact with the teenage giant and let out an almighty BONG. That awoke the giant and Bradnock sat up; he burnt his hand on the oven as he pushed himself into a kneeling position. He stared, one-eyed, at his assailant.

"Mum! What did you do that for?"

"For lying about and making the kitchen look a mess." The large female giant was as big as the male of the species but not as hairy. "You know it is dangerous up by that loch." With that renewed concern and affection, Bradnock felt compelled to stand up and give his mum a cuddle. Smack! The punch was straight and direct, her fist landed onto Bradnock's nose with clinical precision.

"What do you think you are doing? You aren't a baby no more. Be a proper giant like ya other brothers, Adnock and Cadnock. You won't catch those two tied to my apron strings." Bradnock wiped the trickle of blood that had dribbled down onto his top lip. He watched as it merged with the rope burns and stains on his weather-beaten hands.

"I was only trying to make you proud, Mum," he stuttered. "I was trying to get the Afanc. You could make a nice coat or waistcoat out of its hide." The mother giant looked at her son with a strange look on her face. It was hard to tell if it was pity or sorrowfulness.

"You stupid boy, Bradnock. It is about time you grew up and looked after yourself." Her face was now one of ire. "You need to stand on your own two feet and not have me getting you out of trouble all the time." Hands on hips, Bradnock knew she meant business. "How old are you now? Eight? Nine? By the time your father was six he had a place of his own, Zeus rest his soul. It's time for you to go, Bradnock." Indignation was all he could see in his mother's countenance. He knew there was no way of arguing or trying to state a point for himself. He was homeless now.

"I'll just have to go and get my things from my room then, if that is ok?" His eye considered his mum's eyes, they were as cold and unfeeling as a dead fish.

"Just hurry and get gone." The words were short, to the point, clipped. It was final. His mum turned her back towards him and that was the last time he saw her face.

"Ok." His head hung low, dejected. "I'll be off then." There was no reply. Bradnock collected the few things he had, wrapped them in a sheet and slung them over one shoulder. On his way back through the kitchen he noticed a few onions and apples on the side table.

Pocketing the fruit and vegetables, he exited the empty kitchen for the final time. His mum was nowhere to be seen.

16

Back to the Job in Hand

Sunrays reflected within the rainbow colours of the new bulb that the little wise woman had planted. The playful psychedelic patterns appeared to have hypnotized the giant. He now seemed to have come back from his dream state. "How are you feeling, dear Bradnock?" Her tones were calming but fishing to find out the state of mind of the ogre. Bradnock seemed to shake himself out of a stupor, mentally and physically. "I'm ok, little witch." He didn't sound too sure, rounding to face Shiara and putting his face close so she could feel his hot breath. "What is up next, I can do anything you ask, Mum... I mean witch." The mistake stood out and gave Shiara food for thought. Giants were renowned introverts and would sell out their own children for their own selfish means. This slip up made Shiara rethink her stratagem. Could this giant be as bad as he made out? He had been bad-tempered and wrecked a lot of the town but he hadn't killed anyone yet, and he had kept all his promises, so far. Shiara was a wise woman who would give anybody a chance as long as it was for the greater good. Did this barbarian, lone giant deserve a chance? It was time to find out.

"All right Bradnock, it is the same principle as the last test but as you can see the bulb is bigger and brighter." Bradnock looked at the glistening psychedelic monster in front of him again and swallowed hard with trepidation. Shiara noted his vulnerability surface for a second and decided to up the ante. "Inside contains the essence of this Isle, the spirit. Whoever possesses the core of the bulb will not only control the land, they will become the envy of the world. The jewel will give the owner unprecedented influence, not only in this land but all over the world. It might be used for good, bad, greed and influence, but it has great power that cannot be got anywhere else." The giant's eyes lit up and he was staring into the heart of the glassy, vibrant, multi-coloured shoot. His reflection stared back at him, slightly warped and distorted. He noticed the milky eye caused by the Afanc; a sharp imagined pain reminded him of the altercation. His deformed nose that was broken by his own mother looked straightened in the reflection. Deep inside the giant could feel an unstoppable surge of anger rising from the pit of his stomach. Moving Shiara to one side and stepping back the giant readied himself, brandishing the club with wrathful intent. "Where do you want this one to land, Shiara?" It was the first time he had used her real name. She was quite taken aback at first. She could see the rage building in the giant.

"It just needs smashing!" she yelled, over the wind that had started building up around them on the top of the hill. The elemental gale had started to gain momentum from hardly anything but now it was encircling the top of the summit. Shiara wondered if she had made this spell too strong as she clung to the rock that Shanflax, Leo and the water horse were hiding behind.

Bradnock took two paces backwards and concentrated on the shiny reflection of himself which he envisaged as his mum. The anger he felt helped him provoke and invoke the strength needed to smash this beautiful monument to nature. The giant's sudden dash and swing back with his mighty club was accompanied with an almighty holler.

"I WILL SHOW YOU, MOTHER!"

In an immense flash of power and might, deafening sound, a terrific ear-splitting boom was joined with a blaze of white light, as shards of glass shot outwards. The faint ringing was still distinct in Shiara's ears as she dared to open her eyes after what felt like a colossal explosion. Her vision was still slightly impaired and stars danced in front of her eyes. She felt like she had been hit over the head with a plank of wood. She checked herself for cuts and bruises, there were none. She reached her hand into the shadow of the rock.

"Hey, stop it, that tickles," Shanflax protested.

"Sorry, I was just seeing if you were all ok." The shadow shifted slightly. "They are both fine, I'm just shielding them a bit longer. They have slept right through it." Shiara was relieved to hear that. The last thing she wanted was an alarmed water horse and a panicked lynx. She stood, shaky at first, then she walked carefully towards the epicentre of the eruption. Towards where the multi-coloured monument should be standing.

17
The End?

Tiny slivers and wisps of silvery material floated down, spiralling to the ground. The space in front of Shiara was thick with them. Like an endless rain of silvery angel hair. She made her way through the dreamlike grey, silver realm, hands out in front of her, trying to scan for any sign of the growth or Bradnock.

She rummaged inside her pocket until she found a box. Producing the box she opened it and struck the flint inside the box. The sparks flew out from the box and ignited the silvery strands. With a whirlwind and a whoosh the flames caught and cleared the surrounding area within a swish of blue shimmering flame. There stood the multi-coloured ball, proud and glistening in the bright sunlight. Its stem was still firm and as glassy as when it was first created. It looked untouched, complete, with not a scratch visible. The kaleidoscopic lights started to dance and play on the grass now that the silver-slivered air had cleared and the vibrant morning sunshine could penetrate through the bulb.

Shiara noticed the club. It was lying on the ground, split in two. Shards of what looked like clear and brown glass surrounded weapon. Scrutinizing the area around the wrecked bat again she noticed with a start that the glass splinters lay on the ground in the shape of a person, a giant person.

"Oh, my giddy aunt." Shiara was distressed by the sight. "What have I done?" She bit her lip with a tense, strained look on her face. "I don't have this right," she was getting more distraught, "how could I do this to another living thing?"

"Because you had to." The voice from behind was calm and almost whispered. Shiara turned around to face Shanflax, who was now in her solid form, the water horse skating on the palms of her hands, Leo sat proudly beside. Shiara looked thoughtfully into the eyes of the shadow dweller for a few seconds, then closed her own, shaking her head from side to side in regret. She then knelt to the floor; Leo was quick to respond. Back with his beloved lady he curled into her arms, purring and nuzzling into her lap. "Leo, you are a fusspot." The smile was genuine but the tears in her eyes were as well. "I don't know what I would have done if I had lost you." The lynx responded with the warmth of love that could only be felt between the crone and her familiar.

Now sat cross-legged on the grass, facing the glass orb and broken giant, Shiara pondered. Red pinpricks of light from the bulb reflected in her eyes. Then a memory flashed through her brain so fast that she didn't quite get the message. Green pinpricks joined the party of lights in her gorgeous dark eyes, then sky blue followed by a lilac purple. Then all of a sudden all the lights spun in her eyes and seemed to unite into one splendid star. "I've got it!" Shiara jumped up onto her feet in one move. "By the sacred sky, I think I have got it." Shanflax stood back and observed the witch with amusement and quizzical curiosity. "Leo, fetch me my bag please." The lynx tiptoed over to the rock and brought his madam her cloth bag. "Thank you, my darling." The instant the bag was in her hands, it was upturned and its contents spilt onto the ground. There were all sorts of oddities in that bag. Some things that looked shiny and new, some ragged cloth-bound objects that looked very suspect indeed; bits of fabric, shells, twigs, jars, metal of differing colour, pebbles, dried flowers and what looked like a neatly folded satin bag. "That's what I want," taking hold of the bag and hurrying over to the shattered remains of the giant. Amused and slightly puzzled, Shanflax just watched, not knowing what was going to happen next.

The majestic lynx, Leo, observed Shiara; knowing he might be needed at some point, he would be ready.

Kneeling beside what could have only been the head of Bradnock, Shiara produced a flat brush from one of her capacious pockets and began sweeping and collecting the shards, fragments and remains of the giant by putting them in the satin bag. Her audience were now totally lost and didn't know what was happening, but didn't want to disturb her as she looked like she knew what she was doing. The satin bag must have been charmed in some way because Shiara had collected quite a lot of shards but the bag remained the same size, the size of an average marrow.

Shanflax broke the silence and bravely stepped forward and asked, "Is there was anything we could help you with, darling Shiara?" She looked up, appearing annoyed and stressed at first, but then burst into a wide smile.

"Would you all be darlings and go and get Ddraig Dŵr from the cottage." She continued collecting as she spoke. "You could drop off Ceffyl Dŵr at the Wells on the way," looking back up from her task as if only just remembering. "Get Ddraig Dŵr to bring the cauldron, Pair Dadeni, filled with water from wells."

"Ok, no problem. We will not be long." Shanflax, still cradling the Ceffyl Dŵr in her cupped hands, motioned to Leo and they all set off back towards the village. Leo couldn't resist a quick rub against Shiara as he passed her. She returned the favour by patting his head and giving him a quick kiss on the ear. The little troop paced down the hill. Shiara sighed and then returned to the monotonous task collecting all of the pieces.

18

Bit by Bit

Shiara was just picking up the last bit of what must have been Bradnock's right foot and putting it into the ever-expanding satin bag when a terrific roar nearly stopped her heart in fright. She glared upwards to see Ddraig Dŵr, wings spanned out, beating the air majestically as she came into land. She placed the Pair Dadeni, filled with well water, onto the ground with one claw and then landed, curling wings behind her. She lowered the mighty head so Shanflax and Leo could nonchalantly dismount as if they rode a dragon every day.

"Just in time and," Shiara looked at each of them individually, "thank you." Each friend nodded their appreciation of being acknowledged, but all knew the deep gratitude and devotion that this funny little lady had shown them in the past. They would all do anything for Shiara. She was of good heart. "Right, what we need now is to span out into a circle about ten paces back from the cauldron." The group obliged. "Now we need to empty all of our minds of any bad thoughts or intent." They all closed their eyes and concentrated. "Especially you, Shanflax," Shiara warned. "I mean it." The shadow dweller took the counsel and cleared her mind. "Now we all imagine a pure white light hovering above the cauldron; a bright luminous light, full of energy and life." As the dragon, lynx and shadow dweller concentrated, Shiara approached the cauldron and poured the shards of Bradnock's remains into the dark maw that was the top of Pair Dadeni. It seemed to take an age. When she was satisfied that all of the remains were in the cauldron she cast the bag aside, opened her arms wide and walked backwards towards the edge of the circle. To the others' credit they had kept to their absorption in the task. A small orb of light had started to stir in the darkness of the cauldron. Shiara shut her eyes and visualized the light. They all together imagined that light growing. Anyone looking up at the summit of Cleehill that morning would have thought that an enormous mirror was reflecting the sun. A light so bright and dazzling, it built in intensity and became like a second sun. Two shadows were cast out from either side of the hill. The village of Cleobury Mortimer was woken with the pure brilliance of the artificial amplified sunlight.

The gang of four who were creating this brilliant phenomenon were not really aware of the spectacle as they all were in deep, pure concentration. A hum had started to arise from the group. Not orchestrated or pre-empted, just a natural vibration. With the vibration and the power of light increasing a whirlpool had started inside of the cauldron and was spiralling upwards. The mixture of the various coloured glass-like shards were spinning and joining together in a vortex that elevated from Pair Dadeni. The glass-like twister had grown to about six foot in height and started to detach from the cauldron. It hovered briefly within its own turbulence. Suddenly the potency and vigour of the spiral spun faster and faster, then simply disappeared. Vanished. Then from the dispersed spray, as if dropping from thin air, a naked man fell to the ground. The light disappeared, the hum had stopped. The air was still. The group were statues in the aftermath, not daring to open their eyes or mouths. A calmness blew over the summit and in the background the sound of a blackbird interrupted the silence. The circle stayed still, the naked man lay crumpled on the ground.

19

New Beginning

The shadow dweller was the first to open her eyes. With a gasp, Shanflax looked at the prone unclothed person sprawled, then looked around at the group. The dragon still looked like it was in a trance. Leo had lain down and gone to sleep or passed out. Shiara was still in mid meditation, arms still out by her side, palms facing forward. Shanflax knew not to startle a trance-induced person; she crept forward and looked down at the nude figure. She could now tell it was indeed a male of the species and looked normal in size and stature. The face, although dirty from the fall onto the ground, looked normal for Homo sapiens; it had no unusual features or any other creature's traits. It looked like a normal human man. Not wanting to touch the flesh of the newly-created being, in case of any corruption or cross infection due to the enchantment, Shanflax stood, turned and quietly approached Shiara. The dragon had come back into the land of the living and gave out an almighty yawn. Shanflax shushed Ddraig Dŵr, annoyed by the sudden noise. As she approached Shiara, her eyes suddenly snapped open. Startled, Shanflax jumped because of the sudden movement. She could see that the wise woman was still bewitched, as tiny lights still span in those lovely deep dark eyes.

"Shiara," her tone was low and soothing, "are you ok?" No response from the enchantress. "It seems to have worked. Are you okay? Darling?" She stayed statue still for a moment then suddenly, as if a switch had come on in her brain, she blinked, shook her head and smiled sweetly at the shadow dweller. "Hello, Shanflax." She was calm and welcoming as usual. "Of course I'm okay, thank you for asking." Her peripheral vision picked up her surroundings and a puzzled look fell across her face. "Why are we on the top of Cleehill?" Shanflax looked at her, confused. "You don't remember?"

"I wouldn't be asking if I knew, would I!" Shiara was a bit brusque with her reply. Not wanting to have an irate witch on her hands, Shanflax simply stepped aside and revealed the bare fellow lying on the floor next to the cauldron.

Mystified at first, Shiara put her hands up to her mouth.

"What has happened to this poor fellow?" Then the fog in her brain cleared and the memory came rushing back. "Oh, my word. It worked!" Rushing forward she scooped up the man's head and covered him over with her shawl in one swift, fluid move. "I didn't think it would actually work." She looked up at the surrounding friends; even Leo had awakened and come over to snuggle on her lap.

"Who is it?" Shanflax asked, still bamboozled by the appearance of this bloke. Shiara looked at her quizzically.

"You don't know?

"I wouldn't be asking if I knew, would I?" It was Shanflax's turn to be obstinate. "It's Bradnock, of course!" Shiara cradled the head of the new man.

"It can't be!" full of confusion. "He is a man not a giant. Bradnock was a giant."

"I know, I may have altered the spell a bit." Shiara bit her lip again nervously.

"I've never tried it before."

"But that means you have changed his species. How?" Shanflax was getting more and more confused. "Is that even allowed?" Shiara was now getting a bit agonized. "You have played at being a goddess and turned him into something he is not." Shanflax was upset. "I have brought him back."

"Yes and brought him back as a genus that he is not part of. How would you like it if you were brought back as a dog without your say-so?"

"I haven't though, have I. I've brought him back as a man." Shiara lay Bradnock's head down on the ground and stood up to Shanflax.

"As a human male, yes. NOT a male giant!" Shanflax's form was darkening the angrier she got.

"That's good, then. He won't be able to terrorize the villages again." Shiara was becoming obstinate. The eyes of Shanflax darkened and burned with ferocity. "You have taken away his spirit," she seemed to be growing and lengthening, "you have stolen what made him Bradnock."

"He can start afresh, as a man."

"A man, a human! What makes you think humans are so superior?" Shanflax was towering over Shiara. "You humans playing and making pretty things but then if someone else wants to look at or play with your precious things, you kill. Worse than that, humans manipulate other humans and animals alike to support and serve them. What makes people think they have any right over the rest of the living world; chopping down trees, burning forests, culling anything that disagrees with you. Humans are like a disease that keeps multiplying and increasing. Taking what they want and discarding its debris. You even take what you don't need so other creatures go without just to gain control. If there is one species I would definitely NOT want to be, that is human." Shanflax turned on her heel and stormed away, her body shape changing as she went. A shadow drew across the hill as a black cloud covered the sun.

Shiara looked crestfallen as she watched one of her oldest friends disappear into the shadow. Upset, she looked at the dragon that was resting, mimicking the lying position of Leo, which made her smile a little. Leo walked between and rubbed her legs with his head as if to say, it's okay Shiara. Her eyes regarded the new person at her feet. "What have I done?" She knelt beside his head and rummaged in her bag to produce some smelling salts. Unscrewing the tiny brown bottle and holding it just beneath Bradnock's nose she sighed, "Here goes." The bottle was lowered into position and wafted under the ex-giant's nose. First there was a faint twitch of the nostril but then, the eyes snapped open.

20

Eyes Are the Window to the Soul

Bradnock's eyes were wide open and startled. The first thing that Shiara noticed was that they were both the same, no cloudiness. Both eyes were a beautiful emerald green that glittered in the sunlight. The pupils were still dilated and she could still see some shock in the eyes before her. They were open but not registering any movement. Shiara felt worried; what had she done? Was Bradnock alive, dead, in-between? Was he a man or mini-giant or neither? She was beginning to regret her decision. The wise woman didn't feel very wise at the moment. Looking around she noticed that the water dragon had fallen asleep in the warmth of the sun. Shiara knew it was bad for it but she didn't want a grumpy dragon on her hands as well. Leo unfurled himself from the crook of her leg, which he had found comfortable up to now. He looked up at Shiara and could feel her anguish. He then looked at the prostrate Bradnock and narrowed his astute, canny eyes as if summing up the situation. Reversing backwards, the sneaky lynx positioned himself at Bradnock's feet. With an almighty leap he launched himself into the air and landed smack, bang on the mini-giant's chest. Bradnock released an enormous out breath which sounded like a mammoth yawn. Once the lungful of air whistled past the feline's face, he licked Bradnock's facial features from chin to forehead, using his rough, coarse cat tongue to stir and stimulate. It had the desired effect. Bradnock took a massive in breath and started breathing deeply. The lynx padded off the chest of the giant as if it was all in a day's work. Shiara looked on, astonished at the cat, but was brought back to the attention of her patient by the murmur emanating from his lips.

"W-w-w-w..." he struggled.

"It's okay, Bradnock, you are safe." Her delicate hand rose and touched the now smooth cheek. "You had a bit of a fall," she grimaced at the lie just told, "but you are back in one piece now. How do you feel?" Bradnock was looking bemused and trying to take in his surroundings, confusion all over his face. "What happened?" The voice was barely a whisper.

"A big explosion, can you remember?" The ex-giant looked straight at Shiara in fear.

"I remember trying to hit this big ball over the hills and then," he was straining to recall, "whiteness, just pure whiteness everywhere." He suddenly grabbed her hand in terror. "Falling, yes, falling through the whiteness. Nothing around, just pure white, but I could tell I was falling." Shiara could feel by the tightness of his grip that the experience had scared him. She felt very bad for that moment, the feeling that she had intentionally killed a creature and now heard what that creature endured until being brought back. How would he take to being a human? The anxiety was starting to spill out of her.

"Bradnock," her speech was quick and hard. "I may have killed you a little bit." She looked really sheepish and the sentence didn't sound right in her head. "And brought you back to life." She sat back on her haunches as if ready for a tirade of anger. "Also it may have changed your form." Bradnock sat up and looked around. He looked at his hands; they looked a lot smaller than he remembered and clean, with no callouses or hard ugly ridges. It was then when he noticed he was seeing in stereo. His vision was back in both eyes. It had been so long since he had seen through both eyes that he hadn't immediately noticed. He could see the far off hills, clearly. He could differentiate the outline of the fields and hedgerows. He turned his head to face Shiara, who was peeping at him through her dark mane of hair, embarrassedly. He reached out to her with his new, reconditioned hand and elevated her face by her chin so he could regard her aspect. She looked at him, deep in his eyes, and he could have stared at those dark chocolate pools in her eyes for the rest of his life. Her eyes were framed by an elfin sort of face but with beautiful dimpled cheeks. Her hair was thick and lustrous and was the same colour as her eyes. It framed her face perfectly and gave her a playful air.

"You are beautiful." His voice was clear and honey-toned, not booming or giant-like. Shiara withdrew her face from his hand, allowing her hair to fall covering half of it, her liquid brown irises penetrating through the long-haired partition. "You have saved me." Shiara looked up in disbelief. Then all of the pressure in her released. Shiara sprang to her feet and paced, her speech hurried but as if she was talking to some imaginary person right in front of her. "What do you mean 'saved you'? I've changed your species without your permission. What would your mum say, I killed you, brought you back? My cat had to give you the kiss of life, Shanflax has disowned me for playing god, maybe I have? Oh no, I'm doomed. I shouldn't have gone that far. Should I have left you dead and saved the town, or brought you back and hoped you didn't destroy the town? Killing is not in my belief system so why did I come up with this plan? Was it that I subconsciously knew I would bring you back or was I under pressure and didn't know what would happen? I just wanted my Leo back and to keep the kids safe. I don't think I've done this spell before, if I have it wasn't on a living being. Was it on a vegetable or flower?" Shiara was tying herself up in knots, Bradnock could see that. While she was rambling he had stood up, like a new-born horse getting used to long awkward legs, and made his way over to the befuddled lady. She had just finished her sentence when he made it to her and kissed her full on the lips. That stopped her ramble, full stop. After what seemed a blissful eon, the witch opened her eyes, to be greeted by the gorgeous emerald eyes of Bradnock.

"Er," she swallowed hard, still a bit bewildered, "what was that for?"

"For giving me a life. Not saving my life but for giving me a chance of a new life."

"You mean you are not angry or annoyed with me? You are not a giant anymore." Shiara looked puzzled. "Not at all, at least I can have a go at being human." Bradnock tried a reassuring smile. "Look at it this way. I was a giant for a long, long time. Most of the time it was miserable; constant comparison to other giants, tests of strength and the greed that burns inside is overwhelming." Shiara was still unsure and puzzled. Bradnock continued, "Now I am free of that ravenous appetite for domination and confirmation of power. I'm so lucky to have a second chance with a totally different perspective." He put his hands on her shoulders as if to reassure her. "For the history books and the giant's lore, a mighty giant was slain today by a potent witch; the powerful wise woman who protects Cleobury Mortimer. The story will be told on both sides of the divide, the humans' and the giants'. The town will not be invaded by anyone because of the formidable protection of Shiara and the townsfolk will feel safer. A giant should rule a land or die trying; in Mum's eyes, she will have a hero son who died in combat, so everyone wins. Even me." Shiara was taken aback. She hadn't thought of it from that angle. Why would she, she wasn't a giant and did not know what was expected of a young giant. She knew he would be accepted into the community, even if she said he was a travelling rambler lost on Cleehill. The thought that he was the giant who had terrorized the village the night before would probably be a step too far for belief. She looked at Bradnock and smiled. Leaning forward they embraced. "Thank you." He whispered in her ear, she held him closer and realised something was missing. Standing back, looking at him up and down, she realised with embarrassment that he was stark naked. Hurriedly and consciously she averted her eyes and retrieved her shawl to cover him up. Bradnock just laughed at her sudden shyness and revelled in her efforts to make him decent and hide his nudity.

21
Down the Hill

The motley crew of Shiara, Bradnock and Leo made their way down the steep decline of the hill back towards the town. Ddraig Dŵr had awoken from her deep slumber and was flying high overhead carrying the magic cauldron. The revived dragon seemed to be enjoying her new role. She was rolling with the breeze, catching the wind and gliding on the thermals, enjoying the clear blue sky. Shiara was holding her left arm out in a crook so Bradnock could rest his arm through it for balance. He had to hold the shawl together with his left hand to maintain his modesty. Leo wound his slick feline body in and out of the couple's legs with dexterity so as not to trip them up. Something behind a tree caught his eye and the lynx immediately pounced over to the blind spot of the tree to stalk whatever was hiding there. Shiara and Bradnock continued their merry saunter, arm in arm, unaware of the cat's movements. Bradnock was talking animatedly, as if trying to catch up on a lifetime of knowledge. "So, how does this knife and fork thing work, then?"

"You hold the fork in your left hand and knife in the right, jab the bit of food you want to eat, slice off the bits of food that won't fit in your mouth and then put the food in your mouth."

"With your fingers," said Bradnock, eager as a child.

"No!" Shiara giggled, "With the prongs of the fork." She sighed playfully. "There is going to be a stern lesson in manners, young Bradnock." It then occurred to her. "How old

97

are you? Really?" Bradnock looked up thoughtfully, as if to do some mind math. "Well, let's see, I am three hundred and twenty seasons old at the end of spring." It was now Shiara's turn for some multiplication. "You are eighty years old!" Astonished, she stopped walking, instantly halting Bradnock in his stride.

"In human terms, I guess I am." Shiara looked perplexed.

"We are going to have to tell a few white lies to the population of Cleobury."

"Why?"

"Because you only look about thirty-five."

"Really?" He looked genuinely surprised. "That's really weird." Pondering for a second, he probed, "How old are you then, Shiara?" Her cheeks flushed red and she gave that through the hair look that Bradnock was finding more endearing by the second. She then flicked her hair back off her face and stared forward.

"It is a lady's prerogative not to say; it is also rude to ask." She shot him a stern but flirty look. Bradnock laughed out loud and the pair stepped onwards down the hill towards the town, their arms a little bit tighter.

A cool breeze washed over the pair. It made goose bumps rise on them both. The hairs on Shiara's head told her that some malice was about. Unexpectedly, a sort of black covering fell across them. They were caught behind a dark cloth that was see-through and delicate but incredibly strong.

After an initial attempt to tear and lift the binding, the pair quickly realised that it was futile to try. They stood there arm in arm, waiting for whatever had set this trap. "Well, isn't this cosy?" A hissed, almost reptilian, whisper curled around their ears. "The happy couple, bewitched at last." Shiara knew the intonation immediately.

"Shanflax, darling Shanflax, are you okay? I was worried when you stormed off." The shadow dweller revealed herself in a flash of sparkling blue, taking her physical form in front of them both. Bradnock was taken aback by the sudden appearance of a shadow dweller, as he had never seen one before, not for real, only in stories. He knew they were crafty folk, always better to keep them on your side, never ever cross them. He marvelled at Shanflax's form. He bravely spoke. "Are you two friends?"

"We were," spat Shanflax.

"We are," reassured Shiara. "Shanflax please, release us from this binding. We can talk. We have been friends for so long. Please listen to Bradnock's story and then judge us." The wise woman looked directly into Shanflax's eye, trying to pacify her friend.

"Please."

"Why should I listen to you? You have created an anomaly. A non-being. A change in the natural state of things." Her eyes darkened to a crimson red. "He should not exist." The point of her finger was direct and inches away from Bradnock's nose. The dark veil seemed to get tighter around the couple. The ex-giant had never felt dread like this before.

"What do you mean? I am here. I exist."

"You should not." The timbre of the voice was accusing as well as disgusted. "You are an abnormality."

"I'm not. I'm Bradnock." He felt offended by the remarks and found strength to be stern with his answer. The dark material tightened with the increasing wrath of Shanflax. Shiara butted in.

"Oh please, stop it now. This is silly." She was a little tired of being squeezed now. "Anyway, there is one thing you forget, dear friend." Pause was measured for effect. "You were part of the spell, you can't tell me with all of your two hundred years of knowledge that you didn't know that this could have happened. Shanflax," the shadow looked up, eyes now softening to an amber glow, "let us go and we can talk." The shadow dweller sat down and adopted the lotus position but with her head facing the floor, seemingly searching for an answer.

With a rapid flash of movement, a furry assassin appeared from the hedgerow. A sudden keen claw slashed at the opaque

99

shroud that covered the pair, dividing the fabric and rendering the magic redundant. The blur of dark and light pelt flew at Shanflax and, with surprise on its side, it knocked her flat onto her back. Sitting heavily on the shadow dweller's chest, Leo stared into the eyes of Shanflax. Not with any malevolence; the cat engaged her with a disarming, almost cute regard. Shanflax sighed and ruffled the hair on the feline's collar. The lynx immediately replied with a purr and nuzzled his cold nose against the nape of her neck. "Oh, what's the use?" Shanflax sat up, the lynx now sprawling himself across her lap like a lush fur rug. "Whatever I do, it is not going to make a blind bit of difference, is it?" Her eyes looked up and met Shiara's and Bradnock's. They were free from the shroud and sitting cross-legged, smiling at the comfortable-looking Shanflax and her living rug. "It is okay Shan, this happened for a reason and most importantly, no-one died." They looked at each other like old friends. "The giant did," said Shanflax, tousling a long bit of Leo's coat.

"I can live with that," Bradnock interjected, smiling.

"What about the age thing?" Shanflax queried, having heard the recent conversation.

"You are technically eighty in human years. You are knocking on a bit but in giant seasons you are still quite young. At what rate will you age?"

"What do you mean?" Bradnock was confused.

"Oh, I get it." Shiara sparked up and looked at Bradnock. "Will you age quickly with each passing season like a human or, will you continue the slower aging and long life that giants endure." All three were contemplative.

"If you are still of the giant strain, you could live till you are three hundred and fifty-five in human years by my reckoning," calculated Shanflax.

"Is that much?" asked Bradnock innocently.

"It really is if you realise that the average man only lives till he is in his sixties these days." Bradnock whistled.

"That's a bit rubbish."

"It's much better than it used to be."

"Does that make me the town elder?"

Shiara looked at Shanflax and then back to Bradnock.

"In a way, yes." She measured her words carefully. "You only look young so nobody is going to believe your age. You must learn some customs and trades. So no, you won't be the town elder," she noted the disappointment on his face, "but one day you most probably will. We will just have to wait to see if you age quickly or slowly. It's as simple as that."

All three looked at each other and then around at the rolling fields and hills that met the sky far away in the distance. It was still a beautiful day and the sun was nearing its peak. "Better get back to town, we have a little bit of explaining to do, not to mention repair work." Shiara looked at Bradnock like a teacher looks at a naughty school child. "What? Did I do something wrong?" Innocence played all over his face.

"Wrong? Oh my dear Bradnock, you are in for a surprise." Shiara helped him stand and looked at Shanflax. "Thank you Shanflax, you will always be my best friend." The shadow dweller bowed her head and held her hands out in front of Shiara, yellow eyes fixed into her brown ones.

"You are the only human I trust. Shiara, I love you and wish for your happiness forever and for as long as you can remember." A tear appeared in Shiara's eye. Shanflax raised a finger to stop her from saying anything. "I will be there for you if you need me but you will have to give me grace for a while. I have a task to do elsewhere." She curled her hands as if she was holding a ball, a dark movement was forming in the middle. Shiara could have sworn it was a small black spider weaving a web at an unbelievable rate. The ball became a physical ball of matt black material. She turned to Bradnock and let the material unfurl from her hands. It was a cloak. She handed it to him.

"This is an enchanted cloak. When you wear it you will be able to learn skills quicker and become more accomplished than the person who is teaching you. Do not use it for badness or it will repeat that wrongdoing back onto you three times over. Remember and fear me when you put this on because I can grant you this magic, but I can retract it in the blink of an eye." Bradnock nodded and took the cloak as if taking hold of the most precious object in the world. Putting it on he glanced into the enchanted eyes of Shanflax.

"I will not disappoint you, Shanflax, I am honoured to meet you. Thank you." He bowed a solemn stoop.

"One more thing." His face looked up, fearful. "If you do live the long-life line, look after my love, Shiara. She will age at a normal rate. Care for her and she will cherish you. If you live the human life line, please, grow old happily together." Bradnock gulped with relief and looked right and into Shiara's chocolate brown eyes.

"I promise, I will." Another tear appeared in Shiara's eyes as she tried to hug Shanflax but Shanflax took a step back.

"No, darling, it is time for me to leave on my errand." Her shadow form started to dissolve her physical presence. "You have Bradnock to hold onto now." The transformation was complete.

"Goodbye Shanflax, my love. Be safe in your travels." Shiara spoke out into the shadow of the hedgerow.

"I will, blessed be." The voice returned for a fleeting second as it was getting further away. "By the way, he will have to change his name. The town knows that Bradnock was the giant's name." With that Shanflax was gone.

Shiara turned to Bradnock; he stood resplendent in his new cloak, which covered his modesty perfectly.

"She's right, you know. Is there any name you like in particular?" She held her hand out for him to take. He took her hand and smiled. They walked down the path once more. Leo, not disturbed by anything else on the trail, took off on a run into the distance.

"I've always admired the name Tiranatumus."

"Maybe we should think of something less gianty."

"How about Coranathus?"

"Albert?"

"Cradotook?"

"Cecil?"

"Deasmond?"

"Timothy?"

"Aelfric?"

"Mmmm, I do like that." Shiara grinned at Aelfric, nee Bradnock. "Aelfric it is then. That is an old name. It stands for Power-Rule, Aelf-Ric, if I'm not mistaken. Where did you get it from?"

"It was the name of my first pet."

"Really!" Shiara was surprised. "What sort of animal was he?"

"He was a Gwyllgi, a hell hound."

"Why am I not surprised?" Both trotted down the well-worn path towards the town, ready to do some serious explaining.

22

Back into Town

The town was just getting ready for lunchtime. The sound of blackbird song was drifting down from the trees and hedgerows. The new couple walked down the high-street arm in arm. The evocative aroma of freshly baked bread was wafting from the bakery. Aelfric sniffed in the scent and with wide eyes turned to Shiara.

"What on earth is that smell?"

"It's freshly baked bread, why? Don't you like it?" Shiara asked, taking large sniffs of the odour.

"It makes me feel really hungry," he smiled. "I've never tasted bread, is it nice? It smells nice."

"Nice? It's lovely, especially warm straight from the oven." She paused for a moment.

"Wait, you have never tasted bread?"

"No, never." Aelfric looked innocently at Shiara.

"I thought giants ground bones to make bread out of Englishmen?"

"I've never ground anybody's bones, thank you very much." He looked a bit offended. Shiara suddenly realised she may be generalizing a little.

"Oh, I'm so sorry. I heard that rumour somewhere. Something to do with a cow and magic beans." She bit her bottom lip. "This may take a while to get used to."

"It's okay, I understand. I think it's going to take me a bit longer to get used to all these human ways." He put his arm around Shiara's shoulder. "Show me what to do with this bread stuff first, it smells like it has been made by a goddess."

"I wouldn't go so far as calling her a goddess but Mrs Stanwell is a first-rate baker; her buns are wonderfully soft and warm." The joke was lost on the ex-giant; Shiara smiled and pulled at Aelfric's arm. "Come on you, it's time for a taste explosion." Aelfric eagerly followed, his mouth filling with saliva as he was towed to the shop.

The front door gave a little tinkle as the pair entered. Aelfric stopped still and looked all around to see where the ringing was coming from. Shiara pointed up to the tiny little brass bell that was attached to a chain and flicked it with her finger to mimic the door opening. Aelfric cottoned on, but still was mesmerized by the bell. Shiara remembered how, as a giant, he seemed bothered by bells and tore the steeple off the church. She gulped and felt a bit nervous. Luckily his eyes and nose were distracted by the bread. Loaves of different sorts, sizes and colours were stacked on the shelves that surrounded all three walls of the shop. Aelfric was bewitched and dizzy with the assortment of the different shapes in front of him. He went to pick up a round loaf that looked like it had another smaller round loaf sat on top. His fingers, clumsy with excitement, went straight through the crust. He lifted it up like holding a ball.

Shiara sighed.

"Looks like we are having that one, then."

"Good morning, Shiara, it is so good to see you in one piece. How did you get on? Did you get rid of that ghastly, horrible smelly giant?" Mrs Stanwell didn't draw breath or even pause. Shiara looked sorrowfully at Aelfric, trying to say with her eyes, don't say a word. "We saw a hullabaloo and a mighty flash come off the top of Cleehill. I said to Mr Stanwell, I hope that is the disgusting, repulsive giant blowing up and not our darling Shiara." Mrs Stanwell glanced at Aelfric, who was now trying to liberate his fingers from the loaf by eating them free. "Who is this person? I've never seen him around here before." Mrs Stanwell had finally stopped talking.

"Oh, yes you have," Shiara whispered under her breath.

"What was that dear?" Mrs Stanwell was not a lady to be toyed with.

"I said, this is my friend Aelfric, he helped me on the hill this morning." The shopkeeper looked him up and down. Suddenly she noticed that his cloak was open at the front as Aelfric was enjoying his cottage loaf. "Why is he naked?" Mrs Stanwell exclaimed, and pointed, but never actually took her eyes off Aelfric's bare front. Shiara scuttled forward and gathered the cloak at the front with one hand, regaining his modesty. "Well," she was under pressure to get this right the first time, as Mrs Stanwell was a well-known gossip. Once she knew the story, Shiara could be satisfied that it would be around the town before she had set foot back into her own cottage. "His clothes were ripped off in that explosion you saw at the end."

"How do you know him?" Narrow eyes interrogated Shiara.

"He is a lonely traveller who stumbled across me while I was fighting the giant. He appeared, distracting the giant as it tried to hurl a large boulder at me. That was the flying fireball you saw." Shiara was in the swing of it now. "I tried to get an enchantment going and this gentleman, Aelfric, kept the giant busy while I grew my spell. When the spell was ready, the giant hit the ball I had conjured and exploded. Unfortunately, Aelfric got caught in the blast, taking his clothes and memory with it." The baker looked the pair up and down as if processing the validity of the story. "Well, it definitely took his clothes." A little twinkle glittered in the blue eyes of the podgy baker. "Help yourself to a hot roll each and go and get home." Shiara selected a seeded granary loaf, pretty and substantial. Pulling Aelfric by the cloak Shiara led him towards the door.

"Thank you, lady." Aelfric spat some crumbs as he spoke. "That was the best thing I have ever eaten. What was it?" The baker shook her head as he was heaved out of the door.

"Poor lad, must have been one hell of a blow." Tiptoeing up to her own window and peering out to make sure the duo had left, the baker turned the sign around on the door so it said 'back in five minutes', and slipped out.

23

Home, Home Again

The crunch of gravel changed to the silence of walking on grass as Shiara and Aelfric got to the lawn verge that surrounded her little cottage. They paused and sat down in unison, cross-legged, the cool grass a welcome cushion. Tiredness had caught up with them both. Shiara broke the bread and passed half of the loaf to Aelfric. He took it eagerly and started munching his way through the soft centre, leaving the crunchy outer till last. Shiara absorbed the aspect of her home; wattle and daub walls, whitewashed and framed by thick timbers. She massaged beeswax into it every summer when the wood was driest. It had paid off, it was in pristine condition. At night the timbers would talk. A tiny groan here and a creak there were full sentences if you tuned in onto the correct wavelength. At the moment, all she could think of was sleep and her nice comfy feather down mattress. The cool soft cotton sheets and Leo lying on top of her feet, keeping them warm. Shiara had fallen asleep, sitting crossed-legged on the grass. Aelfric was falling asleep too, the last bit of bread lodged in the side of his mouth. Leo nudged Shiara at the side her face. No response; the feline stole away into the cottage, re-emerging a few minutes later with the Robinson family.

By then Mrs Stanwell's gossip had reached most of the town. They surrounded the prone couple and proceeded to gently lift and carry them in doors, passing the slumbering bodies across the chain of townsfolk, person to person, like a wave carrying driftwood tenderly to the shore. Firstly, the stranger was deposited onto the large comfortable straw stuffed chair. After being measured by a dark-clothed man with a string, the group lay Aelfric down. He curled up like a baby and was covered with a couple of woven blankets for comfort. Not once did Aelfric stir, his sleep was as deep as the ocean.

Shiara was being delivered with almost pious respect to her bed by the chain of people. The lady reminiscent of sleeping beauty, but this was pure exhaustion, not a cursed finger prick or poisoned apple. As tender as a mother lays her baby down to sleep, Shiara was lowered into her bed, a crisp cotton sheet placed over her and Leo took his place at her feet, lying down and bowing his head into his resting position. The throng of people took that as a sign to leave. Silently they left the wise woman to sleep a very well-earned sleep.

24

Thanks for the Memory

Sunlight cut through the heavy curtains. A sharp point of sunshine had quietly crept across the pillow until its peak started to touch the tip of Shiara's nose. Firstly, her nose twitched from the prickly heat. A hand idly swatted at nothing and fell flat to rest on the bed. Then the eyelids twitched at the recognition of light trying its hardest to enter and wake up her brain. Shiara flopped the exposed hand to cover her eyes. It didn't work. She was awake. Her stretched arms flew upward until they rested on top of the ornate carved headboard. Her wrists nestled in their usual place, between two carved acorns. With a large intake of breath she yawned and smiled at Leo, who looked up at her scornfully because her stretch had woken him as well. Then she had a flashback. The giant terrorizing the town. The magical bulb that rocketed off towards Witney Court. The shattered giant. She sat bolt upright. Surely it was a dream, a very elaborate one, but still a dream. She peaked under the covers. She was still dressed and dirty.

"Shanflax!" she exclaimed out loud. Leo stood, stretched and then padded off the bed and out of the door. Shiara ruffled her hair and tried to make sense of her dream. Then she heard voices downstairs. They sounded like raised, angry shouts. She nose-dived flat and dangled her head over the side to search under the bed. Rummaging amongst some boxes she seemed to find what she was looking for. It was a long flat box that was brightly coloured with different symbols and strange disjointed emblems. Along the top edge of the box was written, Dyrnwyn, the Sword of Rhydderch Hael.

The Dyrnwyn (White-Hilt) was a magical sword; if it was drawn by an honourable person for an honourable cause the blade would blaze with fire. If the sword was drawn for a dishonourable cause, the blade would reject whoever was holding it.

Opening the box nervously, Shiara took hold of the pure white grip and withdrew the sword from its home. The sword felt good in her hand. The white hilt sat perfectly against her grasp. This reassured her but also made her wary of what lay in store for her downstairs. She edged out of the door onto the landing. Nothing was out of place. The candle was extinguished in the window and looked about the same length as when she last saw it. This reaffirmed to her that all that had happened was a dream or a remembering from a previous life. A roar of raised voices reminded her of the problem in hand. Who or what was downstairs? Leo had gone down about five minutes ago, she didn't hear a sound then. Could whatever was down there have just snuffed out a lynx with no sound? Shiara trod on the corners of each stair so not to make them creak and warn the foe of her coming. A piercing scream that sounded like a child, a loud growl followed by the hiss that could only have come from Leo, made up Shiara's mind in a fraction of a second. She bolted down the stairs and crashed through the kitchen door at the bottom of the stairs. The sight before her made her reel with surprise. A sudden searing pain in her right hand made her scream as the Dyrnwyn burnt itself out of her grasp. Shiara screamed in pain; the entire room shrieked.

25

Revelation

The crowd of townsfolk had gathered around the kitchen table, preparing a wake-up breakfast. In the centre of the throng was Aelfric. He was dressed in clothes, newly tailored and as clean as a whistle. Around his shoulders, he had kept the cape on that Shanflax had bestowed on him. With this cape he had absorbed a lot of skills already. The baker had just started to put the ingredients together for a cake when Aelfric suddenly was able to finish off the recipe in double quick time with no prompts. The same went for his clothing; the tailor had only got as far as finishing one trouser leg when Aelfric had whisked off a tunic. The children found much amusement when this new stranger shouted out the punch lines for the landlord's jokes before he had even started saying them. The kids roared with laughter at the pub owner's frustration. One child fell off his seat laughing and caught the lynx's tail, which made the cat snarl and hiss. Then Shiara came tumbling into the room, weapon raised and scared everyone with the manic savagery in her face. Then the sword burst into flames at the handle and she dropped it with a scream.

"Ow, bloody Nora that hurt!" The room burst into hilarity. Shiara went a bright crimson and tried to hide behind her hair. Aelfric came forward and put his arms around her.

"Welcome back to the land of the living, sleepy head." Shiara looked up into the blue-green eyes that took her all in, pupils widening.

"So it wasn't a dream? It was true?"

"Yes," Aelfric smiled a kind smile, "thank you." Leaning forward he kissed her. Their soft full lips met. It felt like they should have always been together. "Thank you for saving me." His eyes were honest and true. Shiara smiled back while taking his hand. She turned it over and running her finger along his palm she looked up at him again.

"I'm mort…" Her finger was on his lips quickly to hush him, giving him a look that said, do not say a word. She closed his hand. Staring deep into his eyes she stood on her tiptoes and kissed him again. He responded whole-heartedly. Her hand ran up the outside of his arms and slipped the cape off his back. Finishing the kiss, she put her head on his chest and listened to his heartbeat, tossing the cape onto the hat stand in the corner.

"I think that's enough study for one day." Aelfric felt that his shoulders were missing the weight and smiled at the wise woman.

"I certainly have a lot to learn."

"You certainly have." The grin was full and joyous. "Well," she addressed the crowd, "are you here to have a celebration?" The children and adults cheered. "Well come on then."

Epilogue

The froth of the dark beer coated the lush moustache of Lionel. With a wipe of the back of his hand it was gone.

"Well, that's another dome finished. Another good job done." Lionel raised his pint to meet the welder's pint in a congratulatory chink.

"Cheers, it is always good to finish on time." He took a long draft of his pint then looked thoughtfully at Lionel. "What was it?"

"What was what, Mike?"

"That thing we covered over. It was taller than the one we covered at that RAF place near Cromer in Norfolk."

"Trimingham, RAF Trimingham, that was the place. Nice crab and chips in Cromer." Lionel looked lost in his memories for a second. Mike was still mulling over the curiosity in his head.

"But what are they? The objects we have hidden away from the public." He looked worried. "What if they are dangerous, radioactive?"

"They aren't," Lionel scoffed. "They wouldn't let us be so close without protection if they were. Anyway, it's a good screw we are on doing these jobs for the Ministry. Remember what they said, keep your mouths shut and the work will keep coming in. Just let it go, forget about it. I've got Jayne and the grandkids to think of." He looked at the strained welder, then drained his pint. "Anyway, you have far more troubling things to worry about." Mike looked up at Lionel.

"What? What's that then?"

"It's your round again." Lionel grinned as Mike outwardly sighed and collected up the glasses.

"They both looked like giant glass paperweights but dull." Mike paused beside the table.

"How could you tell, you couldn't see them properly because of the cargo nets covering them. They are most likely some old things that they don't want other countries knowing about. Mike, don't worry please." Lionel fished in his pockets for some change. "Get us a pack of salt and vinegar while you are there."

"Okay, no problem. I'll forget about it now. I was just wondering, that's all." Mike made his way to the bar and ordered the crisps and pints. Looking up from the bar he noticed the window. Through the glass he could see the ball on top of Cleehill. It looked majestic, especially as the sun was nearing setting and a wonderful deep red sky silhouetted the monument. Mike wondered what it was and what power it held.

"Two pints of Twisted Spire and two bags of crisps, is there anything else you want?" Mike was brought back to earth by the soft tones of the barmaid, who had just served him. He looked into her dark chocolate brown eyes and smiled.

"No, thank you, that is all." He handed over a note but the lady pushed away the money gently.

"It's ok dear, these are on the house." Her dark brown hair fell across her brow, which gave her a playful air.

"Er, thanks, I don't know what we've done to deserve this, cheers."

"No, thank you." Her voice was soft and like honey.

"What for?" Mike was starting to feel a little nervous.

"For protecting something very dear to us." The lady held up a digit to hold Mike where he was and sidestepped to the door behind the bar. "Aelfric," she called through the opening. "Aelfric, can you put Leo down and come and say thank you to this gentleman please." The bar lady turned back to face Mike and smiled. Mike felt a strange warm feeling but then he heard an almighty clatter from upstairs followed by the heaviest sounding footsteps he had ever heard. He took a large swig of his beer as if he needed some courage.

"He sounds like a big lad." Mike remarked nervously.

"He used to be a giant." Mike looked at her oddly; she just giggled. The door opened fully to reveal an average-sized man. Mike was relieved and disappointed at the same time. The man smiled at Mike then slipped his arm around the woman and kissed her on the lips.

"Have you missed me, Shiara?" Shiara returned another kiss.

"I always do. Is Leo okay?"

"Yes, he is back on the bed, tired out." The couple looked perfect for each other, Mike thought. Why was he standing here, holding a couple of pints, admiring them? Shiara seemed to have read his thoughts as she interjected, "Sorry about that. This is my other half Aelfric," Mike smiled, Aelfric nodded, "and this is the man who has finished the protective casing for the rainbow ball." Aelfric looked at Mike and smiled then looked deep into Shiara's eyes and grinned.

"Really?" asked Aelfric. Shiara nodded. Aelfric moved as quick as lightning over to Mike and slapped him squarely on the shoulders, spilling his beer. "This is wonderful news." Aelfric started pulling a couple of fresh pints of Twisted Spire ale. "That means," he raised one of the pints aloft, "we are free to go." In one swift move the pint was swallowed. "Ahhh, cheers." Mike looked bemused. Shiara produced a tray full of ale and put it on the bar.

"This is for you and your friend." Her smile was illuminated. "Our way of saying thanks."

"We have only done our job." Mike was getting really confused by now.

"And what a wonderful job you have done," Aelfric cheered, and downed another pint. Shiara sidled up to the ex-giant and curled her arms around his neck, taking her face close to his, whispering quietly.

"After three hundred years, does this mean we can go and find Shanflax at last?"

"I think it does." Aelfric lifted the wise woman off her feet and kissed her again. Shiara squealed with joy after responding to the smooch. After a minute of the embrace, she managed to wriggle free of the clinch and run to the door.

"I'm going to pack and get Leonard ready. You," she pointed flirtingly at Aelfric, "better find someone to take over the pub." He grinned and looked around the room. His eyes met with Mike, who was still standing there, dazed by the scene in front of him. The friendly landlord stared for a couple of seconds into Mike's eyes then announced, "The pub is yours."

Mike was taken aback and stuttered, "What do you mean mine? I can't afford to buy this place. I don't know if I want it."

"Do you like the place?"

"Yes, it is very," Mike was trying to find a suitable word but he couldn't, "nice."

"Have you ever thought about running your own pub?"

"Of course I have, everyone has at one time or another."

"What would you do to improve this room?" Mike looked around, he had somehow got caught up in the discussion.

"Well, I would restore the fireplace back to the original and have a log-burning stove put in."

"It's a deal," Aelfric put out his hand to shake, "the pub is yours."

"Now wait a minute. I didn't agree to any sale or anything." Mike had taken a step backwards.

"For free." Aelfric beamed. "It's yours. You don't need to rent anymore, move the kids up here and settle down for once in your life." Mike looked into the blue-green irises of this man and felt his great age, but the man only looked in his mid-forties.

"Why?" he found himself asking. A warm sensation was growing inside of him. The thought of his wife and kids all under one roof and no need to travel hundreds of miles for

117

work pleased him. A chance to set up and settle down properly. "Why me?" Aelfric gave Mike a kind smile and put his hand on his shoulder as if reassuring himself.

"Because Shiara saw you coming and knew you would be worthy." He moved both hands onto Mike's shoulders. "There is a full cellar that should keep you going for at least the next month. All the instructions for deliveries, orders, responsibilities are written in little red books everywhere; Shiara has thought of everything. Trust me, if you are stuck just think of the problem and a red book will appear. Don't ask me how, just accept it."

Mike was in a whirlwind of emotion, spirits, worry and sentiment. How can this be? Then a flashback of a saying his grandfather always said came to him; never look a gift horse in the mouth. That decided it.

"I will, I'll take it." A look of relief took over Mike's face. Aelfric chuckled and smirked.

"We knew you would." The door opened behind the bar. Shiara appeared with an enormous carpet bag. On a lead she had what looked like a dog with a coat on. The dog looked up and Mike noticed it had a cat's face.

"What the…" Shiara put her finger up again and that silenced him immediately. She then smiled and offloaded the bag onto Aelfric.

"The papers are all signed upstairs and the food larder is full. Please continue to be good to everyone and all will be good in return." She blew him a kiss. "Oh yes, there is a group who meet here every full moon. They go into the back of the pub and leave at daybreak. You won't know they are there, you don't have to prepare any food for them. All that they need is thirteen pints of mead which is in the corner of the cellar. You do not charge them anything but they will help you greatly in times of need. Can you do me a favour and continue to give them grace?"

"Of course I will, anything else?"

"No, thank you." With that last word the trio of Shiara, Aelfric and Leo left the pub. Mike looked around and then picked up the tray of drinks. He walked over towards Lionel, who was just about to scorn his friend for being so long, but he had noticed the full tray of ale.

"Holy moly, have you won the Lottery or something? What took you so long?"

"I've got no idea," Mike said automatically, still in shock. "Wait there, I've got to do something." Setting the tray down on the table, Mike turned and headed back towards the bar. Lifting the hatch, he stepped through and stood behind the bar. There was a little red book sitting on the back of the bar beside the till. Mike chuckled to himself. Taking a deep breath he thought, I have always wanted to say this. "Okay, ladies and gentlemen, last orders at the bar."